CROSS PURPOSES

BOOKS BY
JOEL THURTELL

Up the Rouge!
Plug Nickel
Seydou's Christmas Tree
Shoestring Reporter

CROSS PURPOSES

OR

IF NEWSPAPERS HAD COVERED THE CRUCIFIXION

A NOVEL BY

JOEL THURTELL

Hardalee Press

1|12

Published by Hardalee Press
11803 Priscilla Lane
Plymouth, MI 48170

Cover and interior design by Maya Rhodes

Library of Congress Control Number: 2010913331
Thurtell, Joel Howard

ISBN 978-0-9759969-6-6

This book is dedicated to
the American newspaper industry,
whose greed, lust for power, and hypocrisy
churn out a steady supply of rich material for the satirist.

You hypocrites! You know how to interpret the appearance of earth and sky; but why do you not know how to interpret the present time?

— Christ to the multitudes, Luke 12:56

The kingdom of God is not coming with signs to be observed; nor will they say, "Lo, here it is!" or "There!" For behold, the kingdom of God is in the midst of you! — Christ to the Pharisees, Luke 17:21

Don't tell mother I'm a newspaperman. Tell her I've got a respectable job—like playing a piano in a whorehouse.

— attributed to H.L. Mencken

chapter I

JUST A CRUCIFIXION

It was just a flicker on a computer screen, but the blip was enough to stop Caesar's eye. Something about a crucifixion, Pilate and that first-class looney, the so-called J. Christ.

Fifteen minutes before noon, a hot Friday in April. Outside, there is bright sunlight. Inside, the long, narrow Detroit Filibuster newsroom is wrapped in shadows. So that editors and reporters can better read their green and black computer screens, the fluorescent lights are perpetually off. In this cave, men and women decide each day what news seven-hundred-some-odd-thousand people will read and what events don't deserve to see the light of day.

Caesar O'Toole runs a nervous eye down the newsroom's "tickler" file. The tickler is a list of coming events perceived as newsworthy by Filibuster staff members. It is an open computer file, so any staffer may contribute. A token symbol of workplace democracy, it is O'Toole's problem right now: Who, he wondered, made this politically dangerous entry?

Inscribed in bright green cathode ray letters on O'Toole's computer screen is this press conference note, written by some anonymous reporter at some time unknown.

WHAT: Pontius Pilate news conference re J. Christ crucifixion.
WHEN: I post meridian Friday, April XXII
WHERE: Wayne County Jail.
PHOTO: Maybe.

Caesar O'Toole is an assistant city editor, or ACE. ACEs at the Filibuster are the lowest level of executive, roughly equivalent to, say, a sergeant in the Army. They are the crowbars used by higher-level editors to move the foot soldiers — reporters and photographers — into action. By definition, the ACE, therefore, is held in contempt by everyone above and below. This is so obvious, in fact, so fundamental a truth, that all who work in the newsroom know it. Except the ACEs.

Caesar O'Toole is as blind on this issue as all of his compadre ACEs. He holds this thankless job solely because he believes — foolishly and falsely — that it's a step toward real executive power at the newspaper. For as all but fools know, there is no such thing as executive power at a newspaper. Of course, a newspaper is not a lonely place for fools, and oh, how Caesar would love to have the status of a Chester Bontemps, the paper's executive editor, or even of Chutney Vipes, the city editor. O'Toole believes it is possible. Why, he would even settle for being in the chair of Don Strodum, the deputy city editor.

Right now, though, several questions romp through O'Toole's brain, including: How did a presumably important news conference called by the governor manage not to be included on the story budget for Saturday's paper? O'Toole looks up and down the newsroom.

Veteran reporter Blaine Monihan, in once loud but now faded green, blue, orange and red tropical shirt, is yelling obscenities at someone over the telephone. A main contributor to the tickler file, Monihan surely must be aware of the Pilate conference. City editor Chutney Vipes is at his desk reading and rejecting reporters' overtime statements. Vipes chaired the morning news meeting. Hadn't he read the tickler? Of course, O'Toole knows better than to ask whether the city editor had shirked a duty he so obviously should have performed. People who asked questions like that wound up covering Detroit's nighttime police beat, a well-tested purgatory. Caesar shudders. Best to assume — pretend — Vipes knows about this crucifixion.

Vipes knows it, Vipes blows it.

Not worth covering.

Not news.

Or at least not news at the Detroit Filibuster.

Just as well, O'Toole thinks, because it would be hard to shake a city desk reporter loose for an assignment right now, just as most of those vermin were heading out on long Friday lunch breaks.

O'Toole's eyes fall back on the screen. He rereads the little note about Pilate. Again, he feels uneasy. He is downright nervous. What if the unthinkable has happened, and the all-knowing Chutney Vipes indeed has not seen that little notice?

It had happened before. The consequences were predictable. Inevitably, editors at the rival Detroit News and Free Press would see this crucifixion as news and send a reporter out to cover it.

Inevitably, too, David Caninski, the Filibuster's rotund, white-haired little publisher, he who had perfected a seeming incongruity, the fast-talking southern drawl — would read the other paper tomorrow morning while driving rapidly and erratically to work. Caninski would be furious that the Filibuster once again had missed a big story ("big story," defined as such by the fact that the competition had it and the Filibuster did not). In his outrage, Caninski would smash his big black Cadillac into a telephone pole while chewing Vipes out on his car phone, then for no apparent reason, fire the Filibuster's parking lot attendant and two secretaries, while demoting five editors and promoting two reporters to replace them.

Historically speaking, it was a well-worn path.

Vipes, who never got fired or demoted, would nonetheless emerge from Caninski's suite of offices with shrapnel from the publisher's verbal barrage stinging his face, and flecks of cornpone wisdom ("the very duhhh integrity of this duhhh newspaper is at stake here, Chutney, not to mention as ah know ah do not need to the very credibility of all newspapers and indeed newspapering everywhere") drooling out his ears.

Chutney would then charge down to the newsroom and demand to know why he hadn't known about "that Pilate thing." And, of course, nobody would dare tell him it was because he simply didn't take time to read what was in the tickler.

No, some junior editor would be made to pay. Possibly Caesar O'Toole.

O'Toole again surveys the narrow newsroom. Fridays are thin days for staff, but there are even fewer in the newsroom today because many have taken early flights to attend a big out-of-town conference. Suddenly, O'Toole finds what he wants — a reporter who has unwisely chosen to prove his diligence by working through lunch.

It is, in fact, Daley Strumm, the Filibuster's religion reporter. Unlucky, sad-sack Daley Strumm. O'Toole recalls that Strumm had recently been written up in the Filibuster for winning the Orville Award for the Xth consecutive year. The Orville is a much-coveted honor for religion writers. With it came a cash prize, just enough to cover dinner for two at the local chophouse. The Filibuster published a nice little write-up on page IIIA; *Editor & Publisher* took note; the News and Free Press ignored it.

O'Toole had looked on as Strumm modestly and quietly accepted congratulations from his reporter peers. Yes, thinks O'Toole, Daley Strumm is due for comeuppance. Glory goes only so far. And there's another and very consequential reason for selecting Strumm: Who would rush to defend a middle-aged white reporter from any fate O'Toole might design for him?

Strumm will do nicely, thinks O'Toole. There is a saying in the newspaper business: The most important thing to know is whom to blame when things go wrong. The corollary: It's wise to know whom you can get away with dumping on and whom it's best to leave alone. As a handy scapegoat, Strumm is perfect. He would be the only reporter here when the Pilate news conference took place. Not knowing about it, he would not bother to cover it. And for that colossal blunder he would be made to pay. At the Filibuster, punishment was always just around the bend. But to be used only if necessary.

O'Toole briefly pictures the staid religion writer rearranging his personal life in order to accommodate his new assignment — wiping soot off his shaggy beard at five-alarm fires, interviewing mothers of murdered crack cocaine dealers and kissing the asses of multiple Detroit police inspectors to get the scoop on Detroit's nighttime police beat.

Having created in his mind a perfect escape route for himself and Vipes, O'Toole relaxes. No use worrying about extremes, he thinks. Time now to cover my immediate ass.

Half turning his head, O'Toole looks down the row of dark-eyed electronic cyclopes and notes that two terminals away, Don Strodum, the deputy city editor, a thin-faced man with a blond goatee, is munching a pickle-and-cheese sandwich. Despite their proximity, O'Toole shouts, "Hey, Don, take a look at the tickler and tell me what you think about this Pilate gang bang they've got down for one o'clock."

"I saw it," Strodum bellows back without looking up from his screen. He is intently editing a reporter's story, a complicated process the way he does it. He always begins editing by rewriting the first three paragraphs of a story without reading them. This may sound idiotic, and of course, no matter how you look at it, this is the approach of a moron. But there is some technique here: What Strodum does is simply refer to the budget line he wrote before the reporter did his or her gathering of information. The budget line is a placeholder, a little political gambit that enables Strodum to grab space budgeted for tomorrow's paper in a daily catfight known as the morning meeting.

In this little rat race, Strodum must fight with editors from the business, national, sports, suburban and feature desks for space that is constantly being changed either because advertising sold too much or too little. The budget as written by Strodum might say: "Religious nutcase and scofflaw hoist on flagpole. We investigate." A reporter might come back and write that the nut and scofflaw was in fact strung up on a couple of crossed I-beams. This is of no consequence to Strodum, who will pull down the I-beams and reerect the flagpole. Then, his work finished, he might even chide the reporter in a sneering voice: "Your lead contradicts our budget line!"

With a corrected top in place, Strodum deletes most of the original story, still without reading it. "Why use someone else's preconceived notions when mine will do as well?" Strodum once asked a reporter who objected to having his copy wiped blank. Now, with the original story mostly deleted, Strodum gets down to serious editing. Through this frenetic, nerve-racking, know-nothing approach, something like driving a car with a hood over your eyes, Strodum feverishly works through his busy day.

By not looking up to answer O'Toole, Strodum signals that O'Toole has interrupted and further, that Strodum was not pleased by it. One step, indeed, short of being irritated. For this is a difficult procedure, this business of rapidly, furiously moving a few surviving paragraphs from one point to another within a story, then putting them back in their original places minus whatever prepositions, conjunctions and general intelligence had originally glued them together.

When he's done, Strodum will add his initials at the top of the story, denoting that it has been edited entirely to his satisfaction. He then sends the finished story electronically to the Filibuster's copy desk, where another person calls up the reporter's version of the story and begins the laborious task of reconstruction, knowing that the next step is a squabble between Strodum, the reporter, and the copy desk over whose deletions will make the paper.

"What do you think?" O'Toole asks. "It's a fairly slow day — how about sending a reporter and a photographer over to the jail to find out what Pilate's up to?"

"Caesar, if this were tomorrow instead of today and we had a fat Sunday paper instead of a tight Saturday news hole I'd say go for it," Strodum says. "But today is today and not tomorrow. We have a slim paper that's already full. Besides, it's just a crucifixion. If you ask me, we've done crucifixions to death."

"Okay, Don, let me devil's advocate this," says O'Toole. "How many crucifixions does Pontius Pilate call a news conference for? Zero, that's how many. Until now. We could be sitting on a big story here, maybe even a Pulitzer."

A telephone two desks down from O'Toole begins to ring. The assistant city editor sitting beside the ringing phone is reading today's Filibuster sports section. He ignores the ringing, which goes on and on.

All during the discussion, Strodum has been staring glassy-eyed at his screen. Finally he turns to face O'Toole. "Look, OT, aside from one crummy crucifixion, what have you got? That was a story and a sidebar the first time it happened, but the feds have been crucifying people left and right. Now, with Herod in on the action, we don't have the staff to cover every one of these butcheries. Tell me this: What's this one crucifixion got that's any more special than any other run-of-the-mill execution?"

The phone goes on ringing.

As O'Toole tries to formulate a suitably flippant response, Strodum adds, "As far as I'm concerned, the best execution is an uninformed execution. No, wait a minute, that's what I said about the electorate."

Lost for a response, O'Toole in frustration answers the telephone.

"Detroit Filibuster, Caesar O'Toole."

O'Toole listens as a man, obviously very upset, babbles about something, but O'Toole can't make out what.

"Slow down, start from the beginning," O'Toole says, putting on his laid-back, Mr. Easygoing voice. O'Toole listens for a moment, then holds the handset away from his head and says to Strodum, "This is some guy at the courthouse who claims his 'saver' is going to be tortured to death. Says it's an outrage and we should be there, maybe our presence would cool down the cops. His 'saver' is this same 'J. Christ' that Pilate's going to talk about at his news conference."

"Who are you talking to? He trying to sell us a story?"

"I'm not sure — I think he's freelancing for somebody, but he won't say who. Just a minute, let me ask him."

"Hey, uh, John, who you working for?"

O'Toole listens, then breaks away from the phone. "Says he's here to represent God."

"Whew," Strodum whistles. "A geek. Hang up on him. Let's get back to work — we've got copy to move."

"I think we ought to send somebody over there," O'Toole says. "Just in case the News and Freep has somebody on it."

"Baloney, OT — you know what happened the last time we covered a Pilate news conference? He talked for thirty seconds and washed his hands of the whole affair. Forget it."

A tall, angular, good-looking man walks slowly up to Strodum's desk as Strodum finishes speaking. O'Toole and Strodum both wait silently for Chester Bontemps to speak. This is the big boss, the executive editor. Chester Bontemps has presided at papers where Pulitzers were garnered and is widely regarded as something akin to a saint in newspaper management circles. His judgment of news stories is considered flawless.

"Gentlemen," Chester says, "I've got bad news. Once again we've been beaten. I know it's not much of a story, but WWJ is saying Pilate's going to crucify the king of the Jews this afternoon. Tell me if you think that's news. I sort of do. Still, I'm new in this town — do our readers care what happens to Jews? I mean, if we cover this, would we look like milksops or like the sensitive, caring journalists that we are?"

O'Toole's mind races backward and forward as he seeks ways of covering himself. "We just got an anonymous call from a guy at the county jail. Guy says Pilate's torturing some geek to death this afternoon. It could be this same guy who's posing as a king."

"Well, we better have our bases covered on this one," Chester says.

"Right," Strodum chimes in. "There could be a Pulitzer in this thing if we can pull together our local news crew. What's our approach?"

O'Toole, furious that Strodum has stolen his line, pipes up, not sounding nearly as laid-back, "We could come at it from a human rights perspective. Why don't they just kill the guy outright, instead of making him die in agony?"

"Too soft," says Strodum. "We need a harder edge. It's okay with me if they torture him, as long as they let us cover it."

"Who's our anonymous source at the jail?" asks Chester.

"He's anonymous," quickly responds O'Toole.

"Except that his name is 'John,'" says Strodum.

"John what?" asks Chester.

"We don't know," snarls Strodum. "O'Toole thought he was a geek and hung up without getting his last name. All we know is that this 'J. Christ' is some kind of religious fanatic — just what we don't need in these turbulent times."

"Sounds like we should get the editorial writers brewing," muses Chester. "Something along the lines of 'good riddance to bad radicals,' maybe."

Still smarting from what he perceives as a stab in the backside from Strodum, O'Toole softly volunteers, "We're in luck. Daley Strumm, the religion writer, is on hand — perfect guy to cover a religious fanatic's execution."

"Can't touch Strumm," snaps Strodum. "He's writing a weekender comment piece for me on the Druids' Pentecostal movement. I want that piece done and edited by three o'clock."

"Okay," Chester says. "Who else we got?"

All three look over at Blaine Monihan, potbellied, wax-mustachioed star of the police beat.

Monihan is eating a ham-and-cheese sandwich and wiping mayonnaise from his hands onto his faded jeans, carefully avoiding any stains to his blaring tropical shirt.

"Hey, Blaine," Strodum says. "How'd you like to cover a crucifixion?"

"It's been done," Monihan says. "By me. By Mona Mack. By everyone on the staff. Besides, I'm on lunch break. Also, I make two grand a week

— you want your best-paid staffer out grunting around some makeshift wooden cross like a cub reporter? If you do, fine, I'll go. I get paid the same."

"Who else we got?" Chester asks.

O'Toole suddenly thought of Isaiah Perkins, the Wayne County Government reporter. Isaiah has the connections to work the story entirely by phone. A phoner would shortstop all this silliness and let editors get down to serious editing, or at least as serious as any editor can be on a Friday afternoon with a paper so tiny they could all go home and never be missed. Still, though there was much to be said in favor of drafting Isaiah Perkins to cover the cross thing, there's one major reason why O'Toole fails to mention that name: Isaiah Perkins is black.

Moreover, Isaiah is fairly new at the Filibuster, which had stolen him — offering a fat raise — from the Philadelphia Inquirer, which had stolen him — with a big raise — from the Chicago Tribune, which had paid a king's ransom and gotten him from . . . you get the idea. Isaiah is a hot commodity.

At the Filibuster, Isaiah Perkins is viewed by management much as an initial public offering is looked on in the stock market. Various editors had invested in Isaiah, though he is not fully aware of this.

First, Mort Morton, the paper's recruiter, had heard about Isaiah when Mort dropped in on a convention of the Imperial Association of Black Journalists. Isaiah, who knew the rules by which the game was played, and who was hoping to hike his salary well into the six-digit range with another calculated move, put in an appearance and was introduced to Mort. In Isaiah, Mort Morton saw $$ signs. But Mort was competing against the Tiber Street Journal, The New Imperial Times and the Roman Post, all bidding on Isaiah.

Ten weeks of vacation, unlimited compensatory time, free membership in the Detroit Athletic Club, a company car, down payment on a house in Bloomfield Hills and oh, yes, that six-digit salary later, Isaiah was on board and covering the Wayne County beat more or less when and if he wanted to.

You might ask whether editors were carrying out their fiduciary duties to holders of shares in the Detroit Filibuster by giving away the farm in this manner. However, Filibuster managers had other fish to fry than worrying about due diligence. For the next year or two, any editor from Mort Morton on up who promoted Isaiah's career would in turn be promoting his or her own career and more immediately, his or her end-of-year bonus check — a reward for helping to advance the cause of minorities everywhere.

It follows, too, that anyone who might cause Isaiah to mis-step in his collective quest for journalistic success at the Filibuster might be — how do you say? — cutting his/her own throat.

That is why Caesar O'Toole bites his tongue so as not to propose such a logical candidate as Isaiah Perkins for crucifixion duty.

"Well," offers O'Toole nervously, "There's always the Gethsemane Bureau. Calvary's in their territory. Technically speaking, of course."

Strodum does a quick mental check of the Gethsemane staff. There were two white reporters and a black reporter out there, which gave the Filibuster rough racial parity and sure made the News and Free Press look bad on paper, no pun intended. That was a plus. But everything else was a minus. No good restaurants. Cell phones don't work. And oh, yes, staff problems.

One of the white reporters, Robert Saunter, has been exiled to Gethsemane for doing mean-spirited imitations of Dave Caninski, the paper's revered publisher. Strodum suspected he himself might have been the target of such imitations, so the suburban quarantine seemed a just and fitting tribute to this reporter's penchant for being a smart-ass.

Parker Haynes, the other white reporter, fancied himself something of a techno-wizard and claimed to anyone who would listen that the reason cell phones won't work in and around Gethsemane is that some enviro-terrorists are alternately bombing cell towers or jamming their radio frequencies. Really, thinks Strodum, reporters can be such blind idiots. More than likely, it was true. Parker Haynes is no dumbie. He had been an electrical engineer before he became a reporter. Wait a minute, maybe that made him a dumbie, after all. But seriously, look at the paper any day of the week and you'll see full-page ads paid for by cell companies. What newspaper editor with any sense of the bottom line and/or self-preservation would print a story trumpeting bad or nonexistent cell coverage?

But Sarah Bukari, the black Gethsemane reporter, really takes the cake. This is a gal on whom every editor had counted for at least an X-percent-of-salary raise based on the reporter's outstanding performance.

She was a double asterisk — black and female. With a name like that, I mean, it was a no-brainer that she was African American, like a big billboard proclaiming racial opportunity! You could claim affirmative action credit for racial and gender sensitivity. Sarah's job was simply to go along, float, do what she was told, don't make waves, pick up her raises, plum assignments, and lunches at the Rattlesnake Club with Mort, Don, Chester and Dave. And keep her mouth shut.

Yet she just didn't get it. All that was expected were a few softheaded, mush-minded feature stories, yet this reporter kept popping scoops about Herod, a brother, for deuce's sake, and how he was shaking down Detroit city vendors for kickbacks on contracts. Why would a black reporter turn on an elected black mayor? Where was her sense of solidarity with her race? Well, if she couldn't keep her priorities in mind, there were more responsible minds at the paper who would make her toe the line. Oh sure, it was potentially great watchdog journalism, except that it was also an incredible betrayal of those editors who put her in the catbird seat, biting the hand that fed her and her bosses, and, by gum, she deserved the Siberia treatment and then some.

"We've got three reporters in Gethsemane," says Strodum. "Any one of them is capable of reporting this thing, but the problem is, if it turns out to be front page and we give it to a boondocks bureau, stars like Peg Morris and Marty Montecarlo will be pissed that we passed them over. Can we take that risk?"

"Well," says Bontemps, who is well-known throughout the newspaper profession as a man of quick, final and correct decision, "maybe we better just give it to Marty Mont — "

Bontemps pauses, seems to think deeply. His handsome, rough-hewn features concentrate, his lips pucker, a pair of deep, decisive lines furrow his brow.

"On the other hand — "

Just then, a small, buxom, blue-eyed woman with wild-flying black hair and three cameras slung over her shoulder walks up to the city desk and begins spitting words at Bontemps between noisy chomps on bubble gum.

"Hey," says award-winning Filibuster photographer Carla Strumpff, "you guys hear about the big crucifixion? Correction, crucifixionszzz. Plural. Pilate's gonna hang three guys out to dry, and one of 'em he's gonna nail up with big railroad spikes. I shot the spikes already — took a state trooper out to lunch and he showed me the nails — had 'em in the trunk of his squad car, can you believe that? He's gonna sneak me into the carpenter's shop where they're banging out three big crosses, rugged mothers. We're talking exclusive color pics here and a big, big spread, I hope you understand. But here's the prob: I need some reporters out there to do some legwork — talk to the families; you know, the usual sentimental pap to sort of flesh out the pictures. By the way, two of these guys are just thieves, and this seems like pretty stiff medicine for them. The other guy's on some religious bender or whatnot — kind of hard to empathize with. But you can identify with these two poor geezers getting offed just because they heisted some cash from a VII-Eleven. In fact, injustice — that's the angle you should take on this. Anyway, I sent boxes of fresh fruit — oranges and apples and grapes — to the families of these two guys, and in return they agreed to talk only to us and let me shoot their sons through each phase of the crucifixion."

"You cut a deal with the fanatic?" asks Strodum.

"You kidding? What for? He and his whole tribe are very much on the outs with the state police, with Pilate, with the courts, the Pharisees and everybody that counts. If we cut a deal with him, we'd piss off everybody we need for this story. Besides, we don't need to cut a deal with him." Carla Strumpff's face breaks into a broad smile. "He's not going anywhere once he's pinned to that cross. I'll catch him with a long telephoto if I have to, whether he and his kin like it or not."

"Well . . . " Bontemps smiles. "Good. Good. That's what brings in the awards. Now we need a reporter — "

"Yes, for sure, definitely we need a reporter," says Carla. "I admit this kook is getting a tough break, but to tell you the truth, I talk to a guy like that, I get depressed, and it puts me out of the creative mood, you know. Can't be objective."

"I don't think we should write this guy off just yet," Bontemps says. "Let's make sure we get a reporter in there, or up there or out there to get close to the guy, maybe take him out to lunch, build up his trust in us. Maybe that way we can get an exclusive interview and really kick the News and Free Press' ass."

"Right," says Strodum. "Do everything short of pay him. But the key thing is to talk to him and shoot him right when they put those nails in. What's it feel like getting pinned to those boards? Did he ever collect insects as a kid? Pin them to cardboard? Regret it now? What about being a fanatic? Is it worth it? Would he do it all over again? Does it pay to be a religious nut and if so is it union scale?"

"Well," says Bontemps, "those are neat questions, and as usual, you folks are shining under adverse pressure. I admire you. But I lean more to a crowd reaction story. How does John Q. Citizen feel about crucifixion? Is it solving the crime problem or adding to it? Talk to some criminals: Is crucifixion doing its job and deterring them from their lives of crime?"

"If they're criminals, they must not be deterred," says a broad-shouldered man with a heavy brown beard. This is Chutney Vipes, as city editor theoretically subordinate to Bontemps, the executive editor. But for some reason that is hard to understand because of Bontemps' national prestige as an aggressive, award-winning journalist, it is Chutney Vipes who calls shots in the newsroom. Of course, it does no harm that Vipes is dating Minky Maloney, the powerful Filibuster features editor. But is that the only reason why Bontemps' sun seems in near-total eclipse at the Filibuster?

"Well, Chutney," says Bontemps, "I just want it on record that I opt for the high road on this one — no tabloid-style tear-jerking. Now, back to basics, kids: Who's going to report this thing?"

"O'Toole," says Vipes. "O'Toole will report it."

"O'Toole's an editor," says Bontemps.

"O'Toole will report it because he's an editor," says Vipes. "O'Toole will report this because he's an editor with almost no experience at working the other side of the cursor. Also, I wouldn't waste a real reporter's time on this — it's a trite nonstory we're being forced to cover only because the competition might be doing it. I seriously doubt this will even amount to a story. More likely it's a brief with two lines saying so-and-so was crucified and died on the cross and how long it took for him to expire."

"Hey!" exclaims Strodum. "That's an angle: How long does it take for him to die? Wait a minute." Strodum thumbs through a book and continues, "I just looked it up in Guinness World Records, and they don't even have a category for crucifixion. How about we give Guinness a call

— maybe we can get this 'J. Christ' into the Guinness Book under longest lingering death on a cross!"

"I like it," exclaims O'Toole, who has been silent since his name was mentioned in connection with a reporting chore. "It's a perfect, natural way to bring Sports into the loop. It's a ready-made story for Sports to report — "

"Now we're cookin', kids!" Bontemps cuts in, rubbing his hands together and smacking his lips. "I smell the stuff of which Pulitzers are made, fellows. I sense — stop me if I'm wrong — but I sense that we're on our way to making — repeat, I said making — journalistic history here, lads. We take a geek, a nut, a run-of-the-mill fruitcake religious fringe fanatic about to get the big spike and die the death of an obscure martyr. We hoist his name into front-page headlines and bingo — he goes down in history. All because of us."

chapter II

EXPENDABLE

It would not be overstating to say that Caesar O'Toole was extremely unhappy about his assignment to report the crucifixion. Upset, angry, bitter are mild words that hardly describe the way he felt. Of course, the assistant city editor would have felt all of those emotions upon receiving any order requiring him to leave the tall Gothic Filibuster building near the center of Detroit and hustle at a menial news assignment.

To O'Toole's way of thinking, reporting was a role beneath dignity, suitable for half-educated, unambitious bunglers who lack the drive toward a higher calling — namely editing. O'Toole would not have told his true feelings to anybody in the newspaper industry, but if you had asked him what he really thought about those animals, the reporters and their hybrid, mechanized kin the photographers, and if you were a manager in some line of business besides publishing, here is how O'Toole would have responded:

To do their jobs, he would say, reporters are required to talk with criminals of every known type and class, including those presently in jail, such as rapists, murderers, embezzlers, bank robbers, burglars and congressmen. And in addition, they must rub shoulders and even ingratiate themselves with those criminals who are not yet in jail, such as those on trial for heinous crimes and those fish not yet brought in by the wide-swinging net of law enforcement. These would include cops, mayors, state legislators, bar owners, lawyers and television evangelists — and yes, even reporters. O'Toole felt certain that some of the reporters he directed were inherently criminals, even if they had committed no illicit acts.

In a word, reporters worked with scum. And to associate with rabble, mongrel social elements, was to devalue oneself and to become, in spirit if not in fact, riffraff, canaille. Therefore, reporters were all those things, too. And more. They were tiresome, boring, egotistical spoiled brats, in O'Toole's view.

What made matters worse, as far as his self-esteem was concerned, was the fact that his assignment was to cover a crucifixion. No matter that Chutney Vipes had taken him aside and assured him the job was part of Vipes' plan to provide O'Toole with the proper "seasoning" to make him a superb city editor someday. He just plain didn't like being sent out to report what he knew in Vipes' eyes was a minor league execution not worth a full-blown story. He was dead sure that there would be no byline, and no matter how well he covered the event it would be relegated to what editors and reporters alike contemptuously called a "dateline." He could write it now: CALVARY — A penny-ante religious goofball died the martyr's death Friday in the (fill in the correct ordinal number of crucifixions here) cross execution conducted this year.

Since O'Toole had never done any reporting, he couldn't make this prediction from firsthand experience of having watched his writing suffer such humiliating and demoralizing treatment. But he was nevertheless certain it would happen because he had done it so often to reporters. Gleefully.

In fact, Caesar O'Toole's motto, "You can't kill a story," had become an item of folklore amongst Filibuster editorial staff.

An Air Force B-I bomber had crashed in the Porcupine Mountains of Michigan's Upper Peninsula, and star reporter Babe Everest had been assigned to report the story. Luckily for the Air Force, which was trying to keep a lid on the crash, it was late October and near the end of the paper's fiscal year. Hence, the Filibuster was undergoing its annual rite of austerity. The travel budget was on hold until January I — except for exceptions, of course.

Star reporters, photographers and columnists — those who were in favor with top management and whose careers were being promoted as a sort of low-key advertising — could still go where they wanted, and hang the cost.

But that is very general. Let's be more specific: If Chester Bontemps suddenly awoke from the slumber that had propelled him through his career and discovered there was a convention of the Cisallegheny Association of Executive Editors to be convened in Venice, Italy, somehow the bean counters who routinely bounce reporters' expense requests would scrape together the twenty grand Bontemps wanted for first-class air fare, five-star hotels and meals, not to mention a fleet of gondolas for what amounted to a paid vacation on the Adriatic.

But Babe Everest at the time was out of favor because of the affair he was having with Barb "Boing" Alcott, the paper's Detroit City Council reporter. Not that affairs between editorial folks were uncommon — they were condoned in most cases. Top editors had been known to walk into little-used offices only to discover a star reporter copulating with a pressman. Little was thought of this, since a star reporter is like an artist and more or less above the laws of normal humankind.

However, Babe's case was different. His wife was also a Filibuster reporter and worked at a terminal only two desks away from Boing Alcott. Therefore, when Babe accidentally (though there is a dispute about this point) sent all the love letters he had written to Boing to the main city desk computer file, word of the affair tore like thunder through the building and somehow was conducted instantly down the street to the rival Detroit News and Free Press, where hands were rubbed in delight at Babe's folly.

To say the least, the situation was very awkward, made more so by the proximity of Babe, Boing and Billie Mae, Babe's wife. Plus there was the problem of Dave Caninski, the publisher, who wrote weekly columns touting the moral fiber of the newspaper. It was okay to diddle, even intramurally. It was even okay to rupture the fabric of entire families with editorial philandering. But it was taboo to have all three parties at work within fifteen feet of each other with a rival paper grinding out gossip columns about it.

Thus, Babe Everest, a star devalued, was sent to the Porcupines not by first-class airliner, but at midnight straddling a stack of Filibuster bundles in a lumbering DC-III, part of the paper's out-state delivery network. The old prop plane had no seats for passengers and went only as far as Sault Ste. Marie in the eastern Upper Peninsula. So Babe hitched a ride in an oil-belching semi truck dropping papers at every town between Sault Ste. Marie and Wisconsin. The truck coughed oil and roared and stopped over and over that long night, and Babe got no sleep. When he was within five miles of the crash, it was nine in the morning and the driver dropped him on the road.

A farmer who happened to be a longtime Filibuster reader took pity and lent him a motorcycle. Babe had never ridden on a motorcycle. He fell down three times, scraping his legs and feet.

Once arrived at the scene, however, he worked wonders with local sheriff's deputies and even Air Force authorities, got an exclusive interview with the lone crash survivor and discovered what he considered the scoop of his career — that the design for the plane's control system was flawed.

The nation's frontline bomber was in danger of being grounded indefinitely. This one had international story written all over it, Babe knew.

Babe telephoned the city desk back in Detroit and dictated the story. What a blockbuster! Caesar O'Toole was editing copy that day, and it happened that the mayor of Detroit, Herod "Old King" Cole, had gone fishing in Lake Michigan without a license and the Detroit media were stomping all over him.

Of course, there was nothing anybody could do to Herod. He was king and mayor and you couldn't touch him. But the editors at both Detroit dailies, none of whom lived in the city, loved dumping on Herod.

Thus, O'Toole looked at the two stories — Babe Everest's international scoop about the faulty bomber and a witty, light and essentially vacuous story about the mayor's fishing gaffe.

Really, there was no great question in Caesar's mind which one had to be left out. A delicate balancing act ensued as O'Toole, who had space for only one story, carefully made his decision. On the one hand, he had an exclusive story about a dangerous flaw in a billion-bucko airplane, and the military was covering it up. Run the story, do a public service. Then there was this mindless piece about Herod which, if it ran, top editors would be raving about for days.

Everest was in disgrace, and besides, Chutney Vipes, the city editor, said he loved the mayor's fishing story. It had flair, panache. Besides, it was sure to piss off the king — a favorite pastime at the Filibuster. In fact, not to run a biting, sneering story about old Herod would have disappointed hizmadjeztee. It would have deprived Herod of calling a news conference and lashing out viciously at his media critics.

Rubbing his hands, O'Toole leapt into the editing of Everest's story. "You can't kill a story," declared O'Toole in his now-famous remark. He was quoting from Filibuster policy that no assigned and edited major story could be removed from the paper. It was a policy aimed at preventing the arbitrary cutting of stories late at night after dayside editors were home in bed. "Yes, you can't kill a story," O'Toole had said, "but you can turn it into a dateline.

"And," he added, "you certainly can kill a dateline."

A dateline, you see, could in no way be considered a major story.

With two simultaneous strokes of his left pinky and right index fingers on the keyboard, Caesar O'Toole dispatched Babe Everest's bombshell to the "spike" file, to be held two hours and erased completely from the Filibuster computer memory.

Meanwhile, his reporting finished and with a warm glow of satisfaction at knowing he'd done a hard job well, and with his banged-up legs wrapped in thick bandages, Everest caught a Greyhound bus and spent the next eighteen hours riding back to Detroit. Early the next morning, in Big Rapids, he got off the bus long enough to approach a Filibuster vending machine. He'd imagined how his story would be played, with a giant across-the-front headline over his exposé on the Air Force bomber's troubles.

Instead, he saw a picture of the mayor, smiling. He was holding a big salmon for photographers to click at.

In shock, Babe Everest stumbled back to his seat on the bus and tried, in vain, to go to sleep.

From the foregoing, it should be clear as newsprint what a shocking comedown, rebuke and utterly traumatic experience this assignment of covering an obscure crucifixion had to be for Caesar O'Toole. Reporters were the ones to whom editors did things. Reporters were the butts of editors' jokes, they were the ones editors depended on to blame when things went wrong. And now he, Caesar O'Toole, was a reporter!

It was very reluctantly that O'Toole departed the sanctity of his computer screen and sought a reporter's steno pad from the Filibuster's newsroom supply shelf. He moved slowly, as one who leaves warm, peaceful retirement and seclusion to brave a blizzard without a coat. All the while, O'Toole was hoping that some miracle would save him from this fate. Perhaps the phone would ring, bringing news of a story that only he could edit.

Now, despite what certain chaff and refuse among the reporting classes might consider Caesar O'Toole's character defects, the man was not without his own special talent. Let it be said right here and now that he had news sense, the greatest prize an editor can possess. He had an instinctive flair for divining what senior editors would want in the way of news before they actually stated it to him. Like the shark, which combines senses of smell, hearing and feeling to locate minute amounts of raw meat at great distances, Caesar O'Toole had radar, sonar and listening devices that told him what Chutney Vipes or Chester Bontemps would deem good story material even before Vipes or Bontemps knew. That ability had moved O'Toole quickly from a low job as copy editor to the intermediate position of assistant city editor without serving an apprenticeship as reporter.

Oddly, except for a few perennial malcontents, the reporters mostly liked O'Toole. He had a way of camouflaging his contempt for them and squeezing it out as sardonic humor aimed at the higher editors. He was thus looked on as something of a sport and good guy.

O'Toole dawdled at the supply shelf trying to decide whether a wide or a narrow steno pad would best serve his reportage of a crucifixion. He knew the little pads would slip into a hip pocket, because he'd seen Babe Everest come back from assignments that way. On the other hand, the broad pads would hold more writing, and he knew Blaine Monihan favored them.

It irked him briefly that he had caught himself unconsciously choosing between two idiots for a role model.

A short, prematurely white-haired, paunchy man in a gray suit and wire-rimmed glasses entered the newsroom.

David Caninski, publisher of the Filibuster, stood with his thumbs looped through his belt and surveyed the near-empty cavern where Filibuster news was selected, written, edited and like as not rejected.

O'Toole looked upon Caninski with a mingling of fear, awe and mystification. No question about it, David Caninski's word was law in the newsroom. Even Chutney Vipes' seeming omnipotence evaporated in Caninski's presence. And even in Caninski's absence the little potbellied man left lingering in his wake a paranoia that had some real reason for being. For, in his office, in his Bloomfield Hills home and even in his summer cottage on Lake St. Clair, David Caninski could monitor the daily, hourly and minute-by-minute progression of each day's news from computer terminals with direct leased telephone lines leading straight to the Filibuster's mainframe. So, at any time of the day or night, Caninski could scroll through the computer directories, sneaking peeks at the next day's story budget, spying on reporters as they composed their stories. He could even make changes or kill a story before the writer had finished writing it.

Caninski, for instance, had this week discovered three supposedly clandestine love affairs by snooping through staffers' personal message files. There, he found a collection of missives so steamy he would have thrown them out his window if only they had existed as something more than phosphorescent blips on his screen. Further, he had uncovered what he thought was a plot to eavesdrop on his cellular telephone conversations and had set his financial officer to pricing voice scramblers.

And he had, to his amusement, found two reporters' novels in progress and a third reporter's anthology of censored news stories considered too controversial, libelous or simply downright obscene to print in the Filibuster. Caninski, who secretly loved obscenity, pornography and dirty jokes, was following the development of this work, tentatively titled "Blue News," and had even arranged for its author to be given dull, short-term reporting assignments in order to keep him frustrated and angry — the two main prerequisites for imaginative writing.

O'Toole, who had three young sons of his own, was mystified by Caninski, who by the age of forty-three had managed to father eight children and had not stopped there. The Filibuster's well-oiled rumor mill, more carefully reported, edited and polished than the real newspaper, was circulating the report — accurate, of course — that the Caninskis were expecting a ninth bambino.

The same grapevine also had it that David Caninski spent at least fourteen hours of each day in the Filibuster building away from his wife. And, when he was not in his office, Caninski was either attending a Red Wings hockey game, watching the Detroit Tigers play, or taking in a Pistons basketball game. Or he was watching one of his progeny play football, soccer, tennis or hockey. Lest anyone accuse David Caninski of seeking rest and relaxation after a hard day of work, it should be pointed out that he never attended any function without carrying a stack of recent Filibusters. As the game went on, Caninski was absorbed in tearing up the newspapers and scrawling with magic marker keen observations, always flattering, over the writer's byline.

"Enormously important topic, Blaine."

"Incisive piece, Babe — long overdue."

"Crucially relevant, vitally important, historic, bawdaciously good."

Caninski's habit of penning these "raves" during every second of what passed for repose was what mystified O'Toole, on top of the fact that the man rarely quit working.

When did Caninski have time to beget nine offspring?

O'Toole was baffled, as were some of the criminal class, i.e., reporters, one of whom had speculated that the publisher kept that pen busy even as he battled against zero population gain.

Perhaps, mused O'Toole, that would explain some of Dave's weirder raves.

"Thumping, thumping, thumping good ending there, Earl."

"Smoothly written, Jane. Smooth. Smooth. SMOOTH!"

"Wow! WOW!! W O W !!!"

After the publisher had finished and returned to his office, did he send a rave home by company courier to his wife?

"I found that experience to be duh enormously satisfying, and duh relevant to the institution we are both engaged in, duh namely the pursuit of matrimonial coitus."

This line of thinking gave O'Toole an inspiration and soon a plan for how he might, honorably or not, get loose from this crucifixion assignment. Caninski was still standing only ten feet away. O'Toole stepped over to a two-line telephone and punched in one of its numbers, causing it to ring.

The assistant city editor pretended to answer his own fake call.

"Hello, honey," he said in a loud voice to a dead phone. "Afraid I can't go to Bobbie's softball game tonight, awful sorry. Being sent out on a reporting assignment. Uh-huh, guess they can if they want. A crucifixion. Well, could be. Well, yes, it could be dangerous. I don't know why me, no. At Calvary. Well, sure, there's always a mob at a crucifixion, and there might be trouble — that's why they want someone to cover it. . . I said,

I don't know why me. Nothing I can do about it. . . orders from the top — Chutney Vipes himself."

By the time O'Toole hung up, Caninski was gone.

The publisher had repaired to his office, where he sat down at his terminal and logged on, tapping in first the code, CANIN, followed by his secret password, ASCEND. Into the header field he tapped MSG VIPES, then wrote a little electronic note to the city editor.

Chutney: Why have you assigned one of our most promising young ACEs to report on a dangerous, life-threatening event such as a crucifixion? You know very well this newspaper's commitment to family values, therefore I want you to send me by five post meridian today a memo delineating your reasons for placing this firm's entire image of a friendly, caring institution in jeopardy. In short, no editor who has a family with three small children as Caesar O'Toole does, should be relegated to covering a crucifixion, now or in future.

Chutney, simply find someone who is expendable.

CANIN

chapter III

OLD PALS

H igh in the corner of a concrete Gothic building once considered tall, but now dwarfed by the federal government and banking architecture surrounding it, is an L-shaped suite of offices assigned to the publisher of the Detroit Filibuster, David Caninski.

In Caninski's outer office, two secretaries — one white, one black, both female — signifying Caninski's ongoing crusade to integrate the Filibuster racially if not by sex — can be seen through glass windows and doors busily answering phones and telling callers the publisher is indeed in but tied up in a meeting right now and may we have your number so he can get back with you.

One such call had recently come from Pontius Pilate, the federal governor sent to oversee the rebellious fiefdom of Detroit's mayor-king, Herod "Old King" Cole. Pilate's intimacy with Caninski was so well known that he was told the truth: that the Filibuster publisher was doing his aerobic exercises.

When he finished his exercises, Caninski took a quick shower in the stand-up stall he had had built into a side closet of his office. Then, emerging refreshed, he walked over to his long walnut desk. Behind the desk, and positioned so it could be read over the head of the publisher when he was seated, was a wide, brass-framed quotation:

I'VE NEVER HAD TWO BAD DAYS IN A ROW
                                        — David Caninski

Caninski glanced at the framed aphorism, his favorite even over the Dionysian Creed, and mouthed the words, smiling slightly. Then he looked over at the glass-covered top of the desk and saw a yellow telephone message slip with this note:

Mr. Caninski — Pontius Pilate called and wonders if you are still up for lunch at the Detroit Club. He has reserved a table.

Pontius Pilate and David Caninski, it should by now be clear, went back a long way together. They'd been roommates at Herod State University, their wives were fast friends, and the two families shared a vacation house on the expensive shoreline of Lake St. Clair. In fact, Dave often said there was nothing inside the confines of law and accepted morality that he would not do for Pontius Pilate. And Pilate clearly felt the same, having gone to bat for the Filibuster when the paper asked old Herod "King" Cole for a forty-million-bucko tax abatement when it built its new printing plant. Some said it was Pilate's threat to cut off federal grant money to the cash-strapped kingdom of Detroit that had forced Herod to give in, but that's a view laced with cynicism and won't be considered in these pages. Also, financial news is boring and has no place in recounting a paper's coverage of a potentially significant crucifixion.

So it was that over lunch Pontius Pilate had an opportunity to explain his quandary — how the supposed radical J. Christ really was innocent of any wrongdoing as far as the feds were concerned, but the Detroit rabble led by old Herod wanted his head on a platter, à la John the Battist. Pilate knew, incidentally, that John's sobriquet really was "Baptist," but you had to go along to get along, and the federal government was not about to extend its imperial grip to local linguistic oddities. Detroit is a baseball town, and its denizens understand best those expressions that have to do with sports. The newspapers know this and translate many important names and ideas into baseball or football jargon. Thus, the fact that John was famous for spiritually purifying people through anointment with water was irrelevant to local headline writers, who were quick to make an erroneous but cute connection to their favorite sport.

But of course, as with all such bread-breaking rites, there has to be a period of foreplay, a preamble, a softening up of the adversary, if you will. So it was with Pilate and Caninski as they commiserated with each other about their respective unruly staffs.

"So how's the duh federal governor?" said Caninski.

"Oh, man, I'll tell you, Dave, this job is more than I bargained for. It's too new. In theory, I'm over everything — IBI, Imperial attorney, state police; everything, even the register of deeds, answers to me. Old King Herod is a cipher. On paper. But then you've got the high priests, the Pharisees — I mean, they're like free agents. Not to mention nut cases like John the Battist and now this Jesus thing. And Herod behind the scenes. If I could just get people working together in harmony — "

"Believe me, Ponty," said Caninski, "You don't want that. Harmony is the duh last thing to strive for. Control duh control is what you want, and harmony, that is the antithesis of control. As long as your duh underlings do what you want, what do you care if they get along? You're better off if they don't. Better they plot against each other than against you. Does that sound negative? You know me, Ponty, I'm a positive duh kind of guy. Here's the positive: You concoct a system of duh rewards. The beauty of it is that it doesn't duh cost anything. We're a newspaper, so we print up all these coupons, say, for a side of beef free or at forty duh percent off somebody's duh imaginatively calculated list price. Coupons cost us nothing — we print them. Then you stage a duh contest. Prizes are coupons to the best whatever — ad salesman, hottest reporter, zingiest headline writer. Being duh newspaper people, they'll mock the whole idea, but they'll also cash in the coupon for the side of beef. And that's duh just the start.

"We're talking training, Ponty, duh conditioning, behavioral duh tinkering, if you will. Most of it is free. Look at the front page of the Filibuster. Ever wonder how we pick the stories we put on IA?"

"Yes, I have, Dave. Sometimes they seem downright trivial and stupid."

"Trivial and stupid duh is not a problem. A duh reporter who gets a story on IA is being rewarded. It costs us nothing, and is the most powerful duh conditioning tool we have. Nothing beats duh the elation of having your half-assed work showcased out front duh where everybody who sees the Filibuster sees your name. It is a major league high, so it's duh nothing we just give away. Oh no, believe me, Ponty, those duh IA winners pay their dues. We had a reporter recently duh who stood his duh wife up on their anniversary all for a IA story. At least, he was duh led to believe it would be IA. Hilarious! Guy worked six hours overtime, wife duh calling every ten minutes from some chophouse where he was supposed to meet her, and just before the presses ran duh we pulled his story off IA. This little parable demonstrates the eagerness duh with which some reporters aspire to put stuff on Page One. That is social duh control, Ponty. The reward was withheld — "

"You basically screwed the guy."

"How? Does he have a contract that duh says he gets so many IA stories a week? Duh, negative! Only one person has surefire access to IA, and we both know who that is. If it were any other way duh I'd lack complete control of my organization. But that works only with reporters and photographers. Only one way to control editors and keep them duh snarling at each other and not at you."

"What's that?"

"Money. Set specific goals for each duh editor and let them know that if they meet those duh goals, they'll get big monetary duh rewards. But make sure the only person who decides if they have met those goals is you. And also make it clear that the duh goals may be redefined any time at your whim. I admit, this does cost money, and plenty of it. But hey, it's not mine — it's the duh shareholders' — and what they don't know — "

"Will hurt their pocketbooks, right, Dave?"

"Speaking of control, Ponty, what's with this duh Christ character, and why is it duh necessary to resort to duh extreme measures to put down this duh knothead?"

"Well, Dave, this is part of my dilemma. And it's why I wanted to meet with you. I was going to hold a news conference to explain why we were letting Herod kill this fellow, but I couldn't go through with it," Pilate said. "At the last minute, I canceled it. I washed my hands of this thing, but my heart is sick," said Pilate, re-filling his wine glass from a $CL-bottle of Bordeaux.

"This mess could stick to me, unless the press is kind — " Pilate stopped himself. He had been going to say, "unless the press is kind to me." But despite his old friendship with Dave, he remembered that he was, after all, in a bargaining position. It would not be good for their future friendship if he seemed like a supplicant. So he reworded. "It could cause me some personal anguish, unless the press behaves as the responsible institution that I know it is."

"Responsible," echoed Caninski, softly, as if trying out the word for the first time. He leaned back in the heavily varnished oak chair and from habit made hooks of his thumbs, pointing forward, like an umpire calling two batters out at once. "Responsibility. Duh what do you in your duh long experience in dealing with the press consider responsibility to be in this instance?"

"David, if not a single word about this episode ran in the Filibuster, I would consider that the height of responsibility," said Pilate.

"I duh certainly can duh commiserate with the extreme sensation of duh angst that you must be duh feeling right now, Pontius."

"Yes. And of course, I understand that what I'm asking may not be possible. I know there are some journalists on your staff who might object, might call what I'm proposing a form of censorship, favoritism, cronyism, whatever. So, if you need to write a line or two so as to mollify those dissidents who believe a newspaper's duty is to report the news and raise hell, I will understand. Just a line or two, though, in a back section."

"Well, Ponty, I duh appreciate your respect for our responsibility to maintain the enormous duh integrity of this newspaper and the credibility our readers duh have come to expect from the duh Filibuster."

"Thanks for hearing me out," said Pilate. "I guess the bottom line to this whole request is that it's terribly important to old Herod that this crucifixion come off without a hitch. After all, he did approve that tax thing, you know."

Back in his office, Dave Caninski picked up a telephone and placed a call to one of his secretaries sitting at a desk just the other side of his office door.

"Wendy, duh you remember when I had my 'two bad days' slogan printed and framed? Recall duh where we had that done?"

"Yes, sir," said Wendy, the white secretary. "Graphics did it for you."

"Okay, duh Wendy. Take this down: 'It is a newspaper's duh duty to report the news, and duh raise hell.' Put a comma in behind news. Read that back to me."

"'It is a newspaper's duh duty to report the news and duh raise hell. Put a comma in behind news. Read that back — "

"No, no, Jesus Christ! Not — " The publisher halted in mid-sentence, confused. Where had he heard that name before?

"Come in here, goddamit, and I'll write it down for you!"

"And whom shall I attribute it to?"

Caninski frowned. Like that name, Jesus Christ, he couldn't recall where he'd heard the saying.

"Attribute it duh to me," he said.

Alone in his office, Dave Caninski went straight to work like the human meteor and workaholic he was. The situation was perfect. A fanatic and no-account religious radical ready to be crucified for his beliefs, such as they were. A mercenary old mayor hell-bent on delivering an execution to keep the public from thinking about their real problems — no jobs, drugs rampant in neighborhoods, murders, rapes and armed robberies at record levels. And to keep them from thinking about who might be the cause of all this, such as namely, hismadjeztee, Herod "Old King" Cole himself.

So, Caninski thought: Top federal government official wants story squelched. Duty to public. Obligation private in nature to old bosom pal. Corporate political debt to mayor for delivering on tax deal. And of course, wife's plans for beach party with governor's wife hanging in balance. Specter of tense, hostile scene at party as Pontius departs in snit because Filibuster ran big crucifixion story. Yes, the makings were here for a first-class, super-duper humdinger of a Sunday publisher's column. Truckloads of angst.

Hmmm, except that on second thought, it might be best to leave out of the column any mention of his long friendship with Pilate or their joint ownership of a cottage or the beach party plans or the fact that Caninski and Pilate through insider tips had together invested in a sure-bet Upper Peninsula gold mine and were expecting any day to be hoisted tandemly into the ranks of millionaires and individually and separately onto the Fortune D list.

And the matter of the tax fix, well, that was private, corporate business. Ticklish. Complicated. You clutter up a column with dry technicalities like that and you risk confusing your readers. Or even worse, you might bore your audience, Caninski reasoned. Too much business news in the paper is not a good thing. Better to cast the column strictly as an issue of journalism's right to publish versus good public policy. That way, the outcome would be certain.

In fact, there were broader issues here. One was the question of what is news. The Filibuster, as a matter of policy, did not assign reporters to cover every run-of-the-mill crucifixion, and certainly to single out this Jesus Christ character for special treatment could open the paper to criticism for selective coverage of the news.

Then, too, there was the issue of good taste. Every day, the Filibuster dished up hundreds of column inches of news copy about violence, brutality and death. Was there not a limit? Would not readers balk — yea, perhaps even rebel — at being exposed needlessly, indeed, even wantonly, to the gory details of an obscure martyr's death?

Caninski knew what he thought, and he knew what he wanted readers to think, or else. But in the end, he would write, "Please tell me what you, the reader, think."

Meanwhile, Caninski tapped on his keyboard, composing a tart little message for Chutney Vipes. He pressed the SEND key, and the missive disappeared from his screen, on its electronic path as a private message to Chutney Vipes' computer queue.

The message said:

Chutney: Cancel our coverage of crucifixion. Print nothing unless wires move it first. Trim wire copy and run as dateline. Two grafs max.

CANIN

chapter IV

READERS WOULD MISS HIM, BUT . . .

D on Strodum glanced down the city desk budget, the list of the next day's news stories, and decided things were shaping up nicely. Very nicely, indeed.

— The mayor was scheduled for exploratory surgery to discover the extent of a tumor in his colon.

— Eight more Detroit cops, in addition to the fourteen already indicted, had been suspended during an investigation into their alleged robbing of crack cocaine dealers.

— A federal grand jury — according to an unnamed source who happened to carry FBI identification and had breakfast today with Blaine Monihan — was reportedly ready to indict a suburban mayor for buying votes.

— A commuter plane had crashed at Herod City Airport, killing three passengers and injuring two others along with the pilot.

Strodum frowned at the last entry. Not clean, he thought.

"What's the latest from the hospitals on the city airport survivors?" Strodum shouted at O'Toole.

But O'Toole was not at his terminal.

Don Strodum liked stories to come quickly and leave just as fast. He hated follow-up work, which entailed keeping notes, files, and clippings of news stories. Hit hard, hit fast and move on, just like Ulysses S. Grant, his personal hero.

He shook his head and mumbled to nobody but himself, "Unfortunately, we have survivors, so this fucking story isn't going to go away."

A copy aide sitting nearby cocked her head toward Strodum, realized she had not heard wrong and began transcribing his remark into a special file she called "QUOTEBAG."

She moved the quote so it stood above a Don Strodum remark from earlier in the week, when Strodum was angry at the legislature for referring a workplace safety bill out of committee.

On that day, Strodum had declared, "I hate these institutional stories — they never die. Give me a good plane wreck where everyone's killed and you write it once and that's an end of it."

Right now, though, just a few seats away from Strodum, a storm was brewing as Chutney Vipes tried to digest David Caninski's first directive to him — the one that removed Caesar O'Toole from the crucifixion story.

Chutney had just returned from a rather long, secretive and somewhat recreational lunch meeting with Minky Maloney. He was feeling pretty good, pretty on top of the world, and what a bummer to come back and find Caninski demanding a memo by five. A memo of explanation. In the Filibuster building, such memos more often went by the name "forced confession."

Such a memo could easily end up being quoted or misquoted in a Caninski Sunday column for all seven hundred fifty-one thousand four hundred thirty-two Filibuster readers to see, he knew.

Vipes was furious. First of all, he recalled (erroneously), that it was his boss, Chester Bontemps, whose idea it had been to assign O'Toole to the story. Yet here was Chutney Vipes taking the blame for a decision he now recalled that he had believed foolish from the start.

Damn! For two cents I'd cut this motherfucking story from the budget. A family newspaper, indeed! A family newspaper is no place for talk of crucifixion! It's not a story, anyway. Chutney and Minky had talked about crucifixion from every imaginable angle over prime rib sandwiches at Carl's Chop House and both journalists agreed the subject was so ho-hum by now as to put most Filibuster readers to sleep.

"The cardinal rule of journalism," declared Minky, batting those immense blue irises of hers, "is, 'Give the reader what he — or she, as the case may be — wants.'"

"Right," said Chutney. "Whether he — or she — wants it or not."

"Is that what I said?" asked Minky.

It is true that Chutney was paying more attention to the protuberant twin shapes of Minky's breasts under a tan cashmere sweater than to what she said. But as matters turned out, Minky was paying more attention to Chutney's big brown eyes than to what he was saying, so it didn't matter.

It all boiled down to the pair of them agreeing, as they always did, on what was right for the paper. Once both parties have agreed to the conclusion, what difference does it make what discussion led to it? Especially if there's romance at the table?

"Anyway, who wants to read about crucifixion?" declared Chutney. "Nobody, that's who. The feds brought it in to instill discipline among the masses. It's here as long as they are, so we're stuck with it till they go. It's not news anymore. It's not a trend because it's already on the scene. It's not gossip. It may be politics, but not the governmental kind we cover. It's not law, travel, leisure, or — "

"Chutney, you know what it is? Really is?"

"What?"

"It comes under my department. Features, not hard news."

"What do you mean?"

"Chutney, it's right in front of you. Crucifixion draws thousands of spectators, therefore it's — guess what?"

"Sports?"

"No, silly. It's enterTAINment." Minky lifted her voice, nearly singing the word.

They both had a good laugh at that, but now, back at the city desk where reality in the form of deadlines and Dave Caninski reigned supreme, the magnitude of Chutney's problem was beginning to depress the city editor. His inclination was to say, "Okay, Dave, you want O'Toole off the story, great — we simply kill the story."

But as happens with most simple, straightforward solutions suggested at newspapers, Chutney immediately began looking for its weak point with the assurance foregone that if he didn't find one he'd manufacture it.

Caninski wants O'Toole off the story. Doesn't that imply, though, that Caninski wants somebody to do the story, just not O'Toole? Thus, if the story fails to appear in tomorrow's paper, somebody will be writing another forced confession.

Chutney looked all around the newsroom, but couldn't see O'Toole. He needed O'Toole to help him find a chump to cover this damned crucifixion.

Meanwhile, Caesar O'Toole had taken a powder. And just as well for him, given the choice verbiage aimed at his departed backside by Vipes, Strodum and Monihan, all disgusted at the idea of O'Toole's being considered too valuable to send on a dangerous assignment.

"Family man!" exploded Don, albeit in muffled tones for fear Caninski would somehow overhear and send him out to Calvary. "Who *isn't* a family man?"

"More to the point, what if he's already out at the hill?" worried Vipes. "If Dave finds out, our asses are a collective haystack."

"Easy," said Strodum, whose calm came from knowing that only Chutney was being required to sign a confession. "When he gets to Calvary, first thing he does is call in. Then you send him straight home to the bosom of his little family. He's out of the picture, as of now."

"Right, so far so good, but who do we send that's expendable?"

"Well, as I see it," said Strodum, "We have a wide range of choices."

"A copyboy?"

"For starters, yes. Give the kid a crack at a big-time news story. Tell him it's a tryout for a full-time reporting job. We don't have any full-time openings, of course, but he doesn't know that."

"No, I don't think so, Don," said Chutney. "Later on, we may have a use for a copyperson. What if our reporter gets arrested or killed and we need to retrieve his notes? We'd need a loyal copyperson to send on that errand."

"Hmm, good point," said Strodum. "Hadn't thought of that." Strodum looked down the row of terminals and saw Monihan busy swearing over the telephone.

"How about our star cops man?"

"No good. We'll need Monihan for rewrite if our reporter buys it and all we get back is notes."

"Well, let's see — there's our environmental writer. That's a beat we could do without, but he's on vacation. Politics? No, we can't run a paper without bashing government. Hey, how about Quinine, the music critic? We could live without him."

"We could, but Caninski's chairman of the Symphony, remember.

Whether we need Quinine or not, we need him. Who else?"

"Well, we can't send anybody from courts — they're second only to cops in the amount of grisly, gory copy they pour out. They fill the paper for us."

The eyes of both men fell on a bearded man quietly reading the Koran in the twilight of the Filibuster newsroom.

"Daley Strumm!" yelped Vipes. He was delighted to have struck so easily on the obvious solution.

"God, why didn't we think of that right off?" Strodum chortled. "The religion writer, of course. The most useless, absurd, ludicrous, contemptible position on a newspaper!"

Truly delighted for the first time since he'd left Minky Maloney's company, Chutney Vipes chimed in, "Not a soul here reads his tripe unless they're forced to edit it. Not a single person at this paper would miss him one bit! Maybe the readers — yes, probably the readers would — but who cares? What do they have to say? Hell, temples don't buy ads — they're just freeloaders, sponges and leeches always looking for feature write-ups, gratis, as if we're not in business to make money. By God, Don, I've always said religious news was manufactured egghead pap and why should we give a shit about it?"

"One thing . . ." Strodum frowned. "You think he's up to it? Facing a mean mob, hotheaded state troopers, martyr-bashers all lathered up for the cross — this isn't priests reading signs out of cloud formations. Tea and crumpets a crucifixion is not."

"Hell, Don," Vipes said with a laugh, "chances are we'll kill this story anyway, so what difference does it make if Strumm can do the job?"

"Hey, Strumm!" Vipes shouted. "Can that book — we've got a real news assignment for you."

As the heavily bearded, dark-haired Daley Strumm approached the editors' arena, Strodum whispered to Vipes, "Hey, Chut, tell me I'm wrong, but doesn't Strumm have a wife and some kids, too? I mean, isn't he a family man under Caninski's definition?"

"That doesn't matter," Vipes said. "Caninski's note specifically referred to editors. He wasn't talking about reporters. Therefore, Strumm goes."

"Good," said Strodum. "Then as far as the paper's concerned, he's expendable."

chapter V

TROUBLE WITH CHRISTIANS

Seeing Daley Strumm, the earnest, scholarly, hardworking, handsome though slightly overweight religion writer, reminded Vipes of a little trick he'd been waiting to spring on Strumm. Chutney liked to think of these little ploys as managerial traps, and he'd set up Daley a couple days earlier with a memo lauding a Daley Strumm story about temple, money and poverty. To be sure, Chutney didn't send the note of his own free will. That is, he chose to send it, but only because Chester Bontemps had shipped a paper memo to Strumm praising the story. Not to be either outdone or beaten, Chutney — having received a hard copy duplicate of Bontemps' note — simply sent a similar paean via the computer, thus making it appear as if he had beaten Bontemps. It made Bontemps look like a copycat. Which, in fact, he was, having mimicked the Strumm rave he'd been sent as a courtesy by Caninski.

So Daley Strumm over the course of a two-day period was the beneficiary of a sort of chain letter accolade as editors sought to outdo each other singing his merits. It was an ego-inflating experience. Chutney never liked such situations to get out of hand — nothing worse to deal with than a reporter drunk on praise. Thus, the second part of the trap: With Strumm hoisted high, Vipes would knock him low with a measured amount of sarcasm or out-and-out harsh personal criticism.

To kill time and make it look like he was busy as he waited for Strumm, Vipes opened a computer file marked "EBG," for Editing By Goals. This was the Filibuster's way of disciplining management by paying handsome bonuses to those who achieved annual goals. Come December, he'd need to really polish this up, and it didn't hurt to keep a running account through the year. Thus, he typed under the heading of Diversity, "We met our goal of ensuring that at least thirty percent of new city desk hires were minorities and that at least fifty percent were women. Of eight hires, five were minorities* and seven were women (Rexroth*, Schtungelmeyer, Padilla*, Jones, Smith, Bukari* and Amarillo*). Through good salesmanship, I managed to hire a top African-American reporter, Isaiah Perkins*, from the New Imperial Times. Also, I promoted another promising black reporter, Sarah Bukari, to the prestigious Gethsemane Bureau. Rough around the edges, she will receive much-needed seasoning."

That should be good for at least twenty-five Editing By Goals points and a solid ten thousand buckos in my pocket, mused Vipes.

He halted for a moment and asked himself whether he might be pushing his luck by characterizing that assemblage of losers, the Gethsemane Bureau, as "prestigious." Well, it had to follow from the idea that someone might be "promoted" to that hellhole. Nobody had deserved that fate more than the uppity Bukari, whose saucy and downright insolent approach to the city editor was on the verge of earning her the ultimate penalty — reclassification as white. It would be a career-ending move for a black employee that would serve her right.

Now, from the corner of his eye, Vipes could see the religion writer moving toward him. As Daley neared Vipes, the all-in-one good cop/bad cop began rummaging through a manila file folder labeled "Expenses." Strumm, meanwhile, had stopped at the supply shelf and was helping himself liberally to a stack of narrow, white-covered, pocket-sized steno pads. Vipes wanted to yell, "One at a time, hog!" but refrained. Chutney regarded Filibuster supplies as his own personal property — to take from the Filibuster was no different than taking from Chutney Vipes. But to shout out now would spoil the effect of what he had planned.

Instead, as he waited for Strumm to approach, his mind wandered to the memo he was supposed to send up to Caninski by five post meridian. God, what horseshit! The whole idea of forced confessions just plain stank, at least as applied to high-level editors. Vipes' face burned, and unseen by him, his ears reddened in anger and humiliation. Here he was, supposedly boss of the newsroom, yet every lackey on duty today had read and probably printed out the memo David Caninski had sent down to the main city desk computer queue. Degrading? You bet.

And it was all the fault of the tickler file. Rather, of one person who had put one particular entry into the tickler. Vipes vowed he would shell out hard-earned money and buy a steak dinner for any reporter, editor or, yes, even copy aide — well, maybe a cheeseburger with onions in that case — who could point to the man or woman who had put that "J. Christ" item into the tickler.

Damn! Vipes thought. But for that little smidgeon about a Pilate news conference, his afternoon would have been free and clear, a perfect field for his thoughts to graze on dreams of Minky Maloney and how they would conduct themselves during and after their date at Carl's Chop House tonight.

Thus, instead of employing his time to formulate a concise, even mildly sarcastic response for Caninski to read, Vipes was frittering away the afternoon on fantasies about how he would discipline the person who started all this "J. Christ" trouble for him. The refractory individual's fate was settled, of course.

It boiled down to two words: night cops.

Peripherally, Vipes could see Daley Strumm moving toward the editors' area. He was now standing beside Vipes' desk, not two feet away. Quietly, Strumm was waiting to receive his assignment.

Vipes ignored him and continued shuffling through a stack of expense vouchers. By now, a second thought had entered the city editor's mind: Besides revenge on the unwitting fool who had authored that Christ memo, the system would have to be tightened to prevent such miscreants from having access to the tickler file. That was it! Secure the tickler!

He began mentally composing a memo to be sent to every department, every bureau, every employee with a password for the Filibuster computer. (Cynics at the Filibuster, of whom there were a handful, called such Vipes memos "All Points Bulletins.") That's it, he thought: I'll lock the system down. Vipes liked that term — he'd just edited a story about a prison riot, and the idea of applying firmness and force and violence if needed on this computer problem appealed to him. Henceforth, only editors — ranking editors, not assistant city editors — would have access to the tickler.

Later, the professional skeptics would say that with one weak brain wave, Vipes had thus wiped out the single most productive computer-age innovation in the newsroom: the ability to pool and organize news tips without regard to the newsroom pecking order status of the staffers who contributed.

Now, turning abruptly toward Strumm, Vipes bellowed, "What's the idea of expensing off a twenty-bucko parking ticket, Strumm?"

Vipes waved a Filibuster expense form with a photocopy of a Detroit Police Department ticket at Daley Strumm. "You think the Detroit Filibuster should be paying for your parking? We've got lots of folks down here, including me, who pay $LX a month to park in the Filibuster garage. I personally don't think we should have to foot the bill for this. What do you think?"

Strumm blinked. He didn't answer. From bitter experience, he knew better than to answer hotly, from the top of his head. That was what Vipes wanted. Vipes' act was meant to provoke him into saying something stupid that could later be used against him. Strumm decided to adopt the careful, slow, precise, rational approach. He would suppress the quaver in his voice and appear even-tempered and mild.

What Strumm failed to understand was that he would have been better off showing rage and giving Vipes what he wanted. The milquetoast act was guaranteed to have on Vipes the effect Vipes wanted to have on Strumm. For when Vipes didn't get what he wanted, he got very angry.

This approach of the reasoning, competent professional infuriated Vipes. Short-term, he was the loser. Anyone who overheard his mistreatment of Daley Strumm would sympathize with the hapless religion writer and feel anger at the mean-spirited Vipes. But down the road. . . He would chalk this up and wait, just wait. This was not the only box canyon, and ambushes were possible anytime, anywhere. Even, thought Vipes, on Calvary Hill.

"I got that ticket on an assignment you gave me last week when I was asked — "

"I don't care who gave you the assignment," yelled Vipes. "Do you think it's fair to ask the Filibuster to pay a parking ticket you incurred?"

"Yes. You see, Chutney — "

"Fine. Okay. That's all I wanted to hear. You think the Filibuster should pay your tickets, great, we'll cover them. That's all. Now I know."

"But don't you want to know what happened?" asked Daley Strumm. "You wanted a sermon covered and the temple lot was full."

"Daley," said Vipes, switching from frost to warm confidentiality. "Daley, I'm going to give you a chance to shine today. It's a perfect opportunity for you to make up for this little peccadillo of the parking ticket. How would you like to cover a crucifixion — a real good crucifixion? We're talking Page One play — be a great addition to your clip file."

Noting that Strumm was not responding, Vipes came about to a new course. "I mean, Daley, that you are going out to cover a crucifixion that the management of this newspaper has decided must be reported. I know it sounds more like a police story than religion, but somewhere in this J. Christ execution there is some faint trace of religion, I am sure. Anyway, we're short-staffed today. Half our people are in Honolulu running up bar bills at the Diversity shindig while white guys like you and me slog in the trenches to make sure we sell some papers to pay for their party. In short, you're all we've got to send. It's at Calvary and should start soon, so better get going ASAP."

"Calvary's all the way over by Lake Michigan, Chutney — a good three-hour drive."

"Yeah, but the feds are running it with an assist from the state police. You know how those people get along. They'll be lucky if they start three days late."

A small, gray-haired man with a goatee stepped off the elevator and walked toward Vipes. He was well-tanned, with pale blue eyes. This was Rob Wolfman, the former religion writer, now the night cops man.

Wolfman cut right into Vipes' conversation with Strumm. No formality, no politeness. "You see my note in the tickler about Pilate's news conference?" Wolfman asked.

Chutney Vipes blinked, staring at Wolfman. So this was the culprit! Chutney felt two emotions: anger and panic.

"Yes, I saw the note," Vipes said. "And I was wondering who put it there."

"Well, now you know, as if it makes any difference who puts something in a tickler file. A tickler file is there to have stuff put into it as long as the stuff is accurate. Any problem with my note in the accuracy department?"

"No."

"Good. Excellent. Then why didn't we have a reporter at the conference? My sources tell me we weren't represented. The News and Freep was there, WWJ was there, even the goddam Metro Times was there. Why weren't we?"

"Simple," said Chutney. "Because I didn't send anyone."

"You didn't send anyone! The most important news conference Pontius Pilate will ever call — the biggest media meeting in Western civilization, and the city editor of the Filibuster doesn't see fit to send a reporter."

"Finished, Wolfie?" asked Vipes. "Now let me ask you one. Let me get this straight. For sure, it was you who put that 'J. Christ' note in the tickler?"

"Of course it was me — who the hell else has the contacts to know five days in advance what Pontius Pilate is thinking? Pilate doesn't even know himself. The Pharisees do all his thinking for him. My sources told me what would happen, and I called the shot and put it in the file. You're the one who blew it, Chut. Why didn't you send a reporter over there?"

"Didn't think it was important enough, and still don't."

"Okay, Chutney, let me come at it from another angle. Who do we have at Calvary?"

"At the moment? Nobody."

"Nobody? Nobody! Chutney, you are the biggest goddam fool."

"Can it, Wolfman. Here are your marching orders: From now on, keep your cabbage-eating snoot out of the tickler and anything else that's none of your business, or else."

"Is that a threat?"

"Read it however you want."

"Well, pray tell, Mr. City Editor, what new Siberian wasteland do you have in mind for me if I disobey your asinine command? What more can you do to me after exiling me to night cops? There's nothing worse in your vast treasury of sadistic treachery."

"You know what the trouble with you Christians is, Wolfman?" said Chutney Vipes. "No imagination."

chapter VI

DRAINPIPE OF VITRIOL

For a Midwest newspaper, the Detroit Filibuster is an old-timer. With a century and a half of daily newsgathering to its credit, the Filibuster is a proud institution whose history parallels that of its native Michigan. Often short on staff and budget, this paragon of journalistic integrity and forward-thinkingness yet has a longstanding tradition of pulling itself together in the clutch. Pulitzer prizes are no strangers to the Filibuster. Indeed, no matter how bitter the internecine strife, the vicious feuds, gossip-mongering and backstabbing necessary to sustain a large metro paper in its daily quest for the spit and bile of society, the Filibuster is known throughout journalistic circles as one paper that comes up with the goods when the chips are down. The helter-skelter comings and goings of individual reporters, seemingly aimless and random, suddenly transform into miraculous single-mindedness of purpose on the front page, as if the paper had a spirit of its own.

Indeed, the paper's present publisher, David Caninski, had written almost identical words just two weeks earlier as he announced his new "Spirit of the Filibuster" awards — fifty buckos worth of newspaper coupons to the Filibuster employees who best exemplify the paper's rare knack for "pulling together in the clutch." These were not penny-ante coupons, either, but tickets to eat at premier establishments like Little Augustus Pizza, Herod Burger, and Pharisee Gardens. Of course, in his blurb copy, Dave had omitted the parts about the "vicious feuds, gossip-mongering and backstabbing," as well as the bit about "spit and bile," feeling that such admissions, while true, might fuel some legal eagle intent on suing the Filibuster wrongly for libel and finding malice where in fact good will and spite were on equal terms. Hard to explain to outsiders, and even some veteran Filibusterers were prone to take things wrongly, as if spit and bile and vitriol should not be normal components in a newsroom.

No matter that some petty-spirited reporter — or was it one of those vermin photographers? — with a quasi-criminal mentality had rephrased — debased, really — those powerfully eloquent words and used them as a caption under a crude drawing of two rabbits named "Minky" and "Chut."

Minky Maloney found the vulgar, malicious cartoon on her bulletin board: "Pulling together in the hutch."

While some staffers no doubt sniggered and imagined Minky and her consort, Chutney Vipes, thumping together in a wire cage, most undoubtedly interpreted the slander for what it was: the kind of vicious froth which, distasteful though it may be, must be kept in a newspaper's stockroom for priming reporters in their dirty task of vilifying politicians, upbraiding government administrators, scorning businessmen and with a phrase turning private citizens into public laughingstocks. As all who work in newspapers know, the drainpipe of vitriol sometimes backs up and puddles on its source, the newspaper.

It is to be expected.

But the overall dedication of purpose found at the Detroit Filibuster cannot be mistaken: It is that rare ability to make sudden decisions in the face of rapidly developing and totally unexpected circumstances. And at the Filibuster, once a decision is made, the staff unifies behind it, united toward the common goal of reporting the news more fairly, more accurately, more completely and more readably than a certain rival staff of derelicts and their malignant mentors at another daily newspaper about five good stone's heaves down the street.

In fact, there is no better example of the intrepid, tenacious and aggressive news busting done by the Detroit Filibuster than its reportage on the crucifixion of Jesus Christ. Despite initial uncertainty and backbiting, once it was clear that the paper's new executive editor, the formidable Chester Bontemps, wanted the story, all subordinates who knew the difference between working breaking news and rewriting obituaries got behind the effort.

So it was that Don Strodum was rapidly thumbing his way through a schedule of commercial airline flights departing from Detroit Metropolitan Airport.

"Shit!" shouted Strodum. "No flights to Calvary this afternoon. We'll have to charter something for Strumm."

Whereupon Strodum began telephoning from a list of flight service outfits in hopes of finding an idle plane to take reporter Daley Strumm and photographer — or rather, as she preferred it, *photojournalist* — Carla Strumpff to the scene of the next day's hottest news story: the crucifixion of Jesus Christ.

"Damn!" yelled Strodum, "Not a goddam one of them has a plane ready. Can you believe that? In a city of sky-high unemployment no fucking pilot wants to work! Jesus H. — " Strodum frowned, then looked puzzled. He sensed there was something incongruous about what he'd just said. What was it? Well, no time to reflect. That's daily newspapering. Shoot first and philosophize after you retire. If you're still alive to retire. "Hey, Daley! Any objection to riding in a chopper?"

But Daley Strumm was out of earshot, listening to advice from the Filibuster's once-upon-a-time religion writer, Rob Wolfman.

"I'm amazed that they want a story on this," Wolfman was saying. "Not that he needs the likes of the Detroit Filibuster to get his Word across. But still, it would be wonderful if we as journalists at the Filibuster could look back over our careers and say we and this newspaper recognized the story for what it is — the biggest piece of news in all history."

"Hmmm," said Daley Strumm. "I mean, you know these people, but you seem so sure. How can you know ahead of time that this will be the biggest deal in history?"

But Wolfman seemed not to hear. "And it would also be wonderful," Wolfman went on, "if at that future time we could call up in our Filibuster library a series of balanced, enlightened and inspired news stories about the crucifixion of our savior. But I know that's too much to expect. I see it's on the budget for page IA tomorrow, but that's meaningless. The track record of this paper as far as the Messiah is concerned is the next thing to nonexistent. I've been feeding tips to the city desk for years now — ever since his story began in a shoddy Bethlehem manger. Powerful stories we could have been first with. The man's philosophy is the real story, but his history is replete with ready-made publicity angles. He turns water into wine. He walks on water. He feeds thousands with a tiny stock of bread and fish."

"Hmmm," mumbled Daley Strumm. "I really don't recall reading about any of that."

"Hell no, you didn't read it — not in the Filibuster, not in the News and Free Press, not anywhere. And you didn't see it on TV, either. God knows why — it's made for television."

Daley Strumm's face suddenly brightened. "I do remember our doing something on him. Yes — an auction his followers held . . . right? He told them to chuck out everything they owned and get ready for the kingdom of God. We came up with the idea of an auction of all those believers' worldly goods.

"We came up with the idea, all right," said Wolfman. "There was never any auction, in fact. Just in the feature columns of the Filibuster."

"Well, I remember a story about his beating up on some financiers — drove them out of a temple, didn't he? And we did a big backgrounder on depression when we heard he was in a sour mood after Herod knocked off his friend, John the Battist."

"*Bap*tist, Daley. *Bap*tist. Yes, we did those stories. You see the common thread, don't you?"

"No, not really."

"They're all negative! We only do the negative!" fumed Wolfman.

There was a lull in their conversation as Wolfman brooded about the Filibuster's penchant for mean-spirited attacks on weaker people and institutions while supporting those who held power.

Daley Strumm meanwhile wondered if Wolfman's obsession with this one story might explain why Wolfie had been transferred from the religion beat to the night police office. The man was obviously off-kilter.

"Anything that makes us look foolish, churlish, violent, ungodly — that's what they print," Wolfman said. "Bits and pieces of the true picture. Never the whole truth."

Skeptical, Daley Strumm hesitated to keep this conversation alive. "So what's the purpose?"

"Whose purpose? Herod 'King' Cole? Pilate? The state police? The feds? Who knows? I can't even tell you for sure what this newspaper's purpose is. I can't tell you why we do what we do, Daley, but I can tell you what we DO do: We rip up, tear to shreds, snickering behind our anonymous little video screens all the while."

"Well, I think we serve some good purposes, too," said Daley Strumm. "We have our warts, but if there were no newspapers, who would put a check on despots like Herod, martinets like Pilate and..." Daley Strumm paused, trying to think of a suitable next modifier and noun.

Rob Wolfman's pale blue eyes stared, waiting.

The look in those eyes made Daley Strumm lose his train of thought, and again the dialogue was punctuated by silence.

"'If there were no newspapers, who would put a check on despots like Herod, martinets like Pilate...'" Wolfman played back Strumm's words, adding, "And maybe you were about to say blowhard accomplices like Dave Caninski?"

chapter VII

BIGGEST NONSTORY

Man, this sucker's a real hard-ass," Don Strodum said. His video display showed a Filibuster library copy of a story the paper had published sometime earlier.

"Here's a story we ran about this Jesus character where the damned fool's telling his disciples to dump everything they own and hop on the bandwagon. Can you believe this stuff? Imagine, here's another story where his henchman cuts a guy's ear off. We're dealing with a hardcore crim — hey, Daley! Come on over here! He better read this copy before he goes out there, so he knows what kind of nether element he's dealing with. This guy's not religious: He's a hooligan, next thing to a terrorist. Belongs in Palestine, or Iraq."

Still muttering to no one in particular, Strodum went back to reading the screen and soon was grumbling about a Peg Morris bylined story. "Talk about a blow job! Jesus, old top-of-the-hill Pat really one-upped herself on this one. Look here, I've never seen a reporter who could milk poignancy out of a corncob like our Peggy can. Can't fathom a guy, let alone a fanatic, who fast-talks his people into auctioning off their belongings while they wait for the kingdom of God."

"As I recall, there was no auction," said Vipes. "We had to run a 'Getting it Right' on that. Morris overwrote that yarn. I don't have any problem with hype per se, of course, but she stepped across the imaginary line. And got caught. That's not good.

"I'll tell you something else: That correction came because of an almighty stink Christ's followers made with Caninski himself. I got burned a little myself, because the auction was my idea, and Morris, pig that she is, squealed it all out to Dave when he demanded her written confession. Burned as I was, I decided to nix any ongoing coverage of this Christ story. Too risky. Christians are just too exacting in what they expect in the way of accuracy and fairness from a daily newspaper put out by overworked chain-smokers, alcoholics and general pains-in-the-ass on panic-stricken deadline. They want to hew that closely to the facts, then fuck 'em, I say. Cross me, I cross them."

But Strodum wasn't listening. He'd gone back to scrolling through microfiches of library files of old Filibuster copy. "Hah! Get this, here's a real thumb-sucker: Jesus sees a shrink after Herod lops John the Battist. Sheer unadulterated crap. Who cares?"

"Nobody cares," chimed in Vipes. "Except, I might caution you, the – ha-ha — expletive editor."

"Well, if you ask me, Jesus is the biggest nonstory to hit since those goddam whales got locked in the ice. What can we do about derailing this son of a bitch?"

"Nothing," said Vipes. "We're stuck with it. Chester Bontemps in his preeminent wisdom and overarching news canniness has decreed that we make it a story. He's excited as hell, wants the whole paper to pull together. Wants Sports in on the act, The Way We Are is working up some sob sister — "

Vipes stopped himself, too late, from uttering a sexist remark while on duty in the newsroom. Recently, an editor had been written up in David Caninski's Sunday column for using the term "weak sister" in a story. The expression was deemed to be derogatory to females, and Vipes now was forced to censor his own speech just to defend against being keelhauled in a Caninski column. Maybe Strodum, whose motto was "So what if it's sleazy?" hadn't noticed.

"Anyway," Vipes continued with a sly grin, "I convinced him to ap-proach Mowat Jones about writing an editorial."

"You what?" said Strodum.

"An editorial condemning crucifixion," said Vipes.

"You didn't!"

"I did."

"Wow! You know what Mowat's going to say?"

"Better than that, I know what Mowat's going to think," said Vipes. "If Chester Bontemps with his prep school V-neck sweater and Roman nose hauteur dares toss an editorial idea Mowat's way, our editorial page editor will go through the roof. News types like us don't peddle our wares in the editorial section. Verboten."

"Right, but that's not what Mowat's gonna say."

"I have no idea what Mowat's going to say, Don, and I don't care. If the executive editor is stupid enough to take crucifixion to Mowat Jones, he will pay for his transgression from then until the brass in our parent company decide Chester has served his purpose and should be kicked farther upstairs where he can do much greater irreparable harm to the noble cause of journalism."

"You're a genius, Chut," said Strodum. "Diabolical, perhaps. Conniving, for sure. Malicious, absolutely. Dangerous, to the core. Sleazy, underhanded, manipulative and cunning. But so what?"

"To coin a phrase, 'So what if it's sleazy?'" Vipes laughed.

"Well, you have my admiration," said Strodum. "I'm with you a hundred percent on this one. You know what my dad always told me: 'If everyone smells bad, nobody smells bad.'"

"That's one to remember," said Vipes. "Now, let's get going on this favorite story of ours: the crucifixion of one Jesus Christ."

chapter VIII

Balancing Acts

The crucifixion of one fanatic assho — " Strodum cut his remark short at sight of the executive editor walking through the newsroom with an immense frown on his face. Nobody could beat Chester Bontemps at laughing or frowning; his long jowl and broad chin were built for both kinds of exercise.

Bontemps was returning from a visit with Mowat Jones, editorial page editor of the stately Detroit Filibuster.

The experience had been, to say the least, degrading, humiliating, humbling, embarrassing — in short, a total disaster that made Bontemps wonder how much of a future he might possibly have at the world-renowned Filibuster he'd striven so long to reach.

Depressing, the meeting had been. Disillusioning also. Disheartening. These were all words Bontemps intended to write into a secret memo he would type — not enter into the Filibuster computer system with its myriad of electronic eavesdroppers — and hand-deliver to Dave Caninski himself.

This was beyond explanation, beyond apology, beyond the bounds of decency, beyond Bontemps' ability to find more pejorative words right now.

Chester Bontemps got no sense that Mowat Jones or his editorial department had any inkling that they worked for the same newspaper as Chester Bontemps, or that there should be teamwork, not mutual sabotage.

Here in a nutshell is what had happened:

For starters, Bontemps had not even been admitted to see Jones right away, as was an executive editor's right. He was made to cool his heels in the editorial department's outer office, which consisted of a rather longish hall in which a few slow-moving employees seemed to be busily exchanging scuttlebutt. A young man with dark hair and a suspicious expression invited Bontemps to have a seat. Bontemps sat beside a table littered with old copies of domestic and foreign newspapers and magazines. Since he could understand German, he picked up a dog-eared copy of *Die Zeit* and began reading. But his excitement wouldn't allow him to concentrate on the foreign words' meanings.

At last, he felt, after six months as executive editor, he had a chance to harness the Filibuster into a common struggle for news. Yet paired with this thought was the faint feeling that this waiting was akin to some local politician being made to hold his fire before the big interview with Mowat Jones, where he would either ingratiate himself sufficiently to earn an endorsement from the paper, or cut his throat media-wise. With Jones, there were no gray areas.

Now, as he waited for his audience with Mr. Jones, he overheard a conversation between Leo Ober, the Filibuster's reader representative, or ombudsman, and a copy aide whose name Bontemps didn't know.

"Weird thing," Ober said. "We've got a crucifixion story on the budget, despite the fact we've got a long-standing agreement with city desk not to write about them."

"Why not?"

"It's okay to cover them as long as we don't print anything — ha-ha. Seriously, they generate too many letters to the editor. All sorts of geeks crawl out and get excited when you run crucifixion stories, and it's all been said before."

Chester Bontemps was amazed. Here were two men — Filibuster employees — technically his subordinates, discussing the paper's policy as though he were not present.

He was tempted to break in and set the record straight: There were no agreements that he knew of between the editorial people and the city desk to censor the news, and these people might as well know that right now. But somewhere far back in the recesses of his résumé was a short stint of reporting. An echo of that long-ago street experience so foreign to most editors throbbed in Bontemps' brain and he decided to shut up and listen.

"Of course, it all depends who they send out to cover it," Ober said. "I see they've got Daley Strumm down. He's a decent enough reporter, fair-minded as far as I know. Better than the previous religion writer, whose religious commitments made him an impediment to the paper."

"Who was that?"

"Guy named Rob Wolfman. Talk about subjective. He was a true believer as far as religion was concerned. Bad trait in a reporter. Shouldn't believe in any aspect of what you're covering. Compromises your objectivity. A neutral observer Rob Wolfman was not. Thank God Wolfie's off religion. He was okay when it was just the temple page, in the old days, before Caninski got the idea of marketing religious news. But give a guy like Wolfman a little freedom, room for a little style, and he goes hog-wild. Every goddam story the little guy wrote, you could tell he had feelings. All the issues things, you know, like female clergy, temple and economics, poverty, civil rights — hell, you don't even choose to write about those things unless you have some sort of belief or value system. So, as I say, he outlived his usefulness to this paper."

"He's still around, though. I saw him just today. He seemed to be chewing out Chutney Vipes."

"In a manner of speaking, he's still around. And yet he's not. Vipes shoved him over onto night cops. No time for values or mores over there. Strictly blood-and-guts journalism. Great story on how they banished him to the cop shop. Of course, he wouldn't go willingly; they knew that, so Vipes waited for him to make a mistake.

"Naturally, given the nature of this business, editors pulling you three different ways, everything rush, rush, rush, a reporter inevitably makes mistakes. Factual errors are easiest to catch, but often they'll piss off somebody who has lunch with Caninski. Some suburban mayor with his hand in the till, maybe, yet socially prominent who parties with Caninski. Reporter doesn't know it, maybe, or maybe does know it and sees some higher duty — like committing hara-kiri, employment-wise.

"But with Wolfman it was even easier. It was like he set himself up for martyrdom. Remember those 'vegetarian parents' stories we were running last year?"

"'Vegetarian parents.' Rings a bell. Parents wouldn't make their kids eat vegetables?"

"No, no, no! Vegetables didn't have anything to do with the story, really. We just threw that into the mix for fun. We made a laughingstock of these people, basically pilloried them in public. But not being the socially eminent types who party with Caninski, they were in no position to make us stop or even shame us. They were powerless, nobodies — perfect targets. So we had great fun, snickering behind our terminals and yucking it up over lunch. What a hoot!

"No, here's the deal: They were Seventh-day Ablatives or some such tripe and wanted to teach their kids at home. Didn't want them in public school. Schools sued to get the kids in class. Whole series of stories we did. Generic, so to speak, class unto themselves — 'Vegetarian parents' stories."

"So where do the vegetables come in?"

"Aha! Thought you'd never ask. The family didn't eat meat — didn't believe in it. Just ate vegetables, or whatever they could find that wasn't meat. That's where Wolfman comes in, oversteps himself. See, he's a vegetarian, too. But it wasn't his story; it was a police and court story. He was the religion guy back then. Nevertheless, Wolfie can't keep his snout out of it, writes a hot memo to Chutney about our coverage, and that's all Chut needed."

"What'd the memo say?"

"Oh, it was classic. I saved it. Hang on a minute." Ober fished through a stack of papers on his desk and pulled up a single typed piece of paper. "Here, read it for yourself."

The copy aide read the now famous Wolfman memo:

Dear Chutney,
May I ask you a personal question?
Is your dick a zucchini?
You got bean sprouts for pubic hair?
And what are your balls made of — walnuts?
I won't ask about your brain, assuming it exists.
Do you think my questions impertinent?
So do I — as impertinent as your publishing newspaper articles about
"vegetarian parents."

What do these people's dietary preferences have to do with the way they teach their young how to read and write and do sums?

If these parents ate hamburger and beer-battered shrimp, would you call them "meat-eating parents"?

If they hung out in taverns and consumed six-packs of beer, would you call them "alcoholic parents"?

If they charred their lungs inhaling the fumes of cigars and cigarettes, would you call them "smoking parents"?

Apparently, it's so commonplace to the media that people ruin their livers with booze, their lungs with tobacco smoke and turn their guts into graveyards for the flesh of murdered animals that you see no reason to label those people for the way they eat abusively and drink and smoke themselves into oblivion.

Why then single out for ridicule those of us who choose not to afflict our bodies with diabetes-provoking soda pop, french fries, liver-battering booze and heart-and-lung-destructive nicotine?

Are you somehow jealous of those with the will power to avoid the self-destruction that awaits eaters of deep-fried foods and drinkers of stupefying liquor?

Tell me, Chutney, what is a "vegetarian parent," anyway? Do the females have onions for breasts, tomatoes for ovaries and lettuce for pubic hair? Do the men have balls made of garlic cloves and bananas for penises?

Why do you think it's weird to eat only vegetables and yet think it's normal to consume meat that has been bludgeoned and shot, with brains blown out, throats knifed, and blood, gore and guts spewing E. coli and salmonella high and wide?

Quit stereotyping vegetarians and you may soon learn to stop putting your idiotic but insulting labels on ANYONE you perceive as a little bit different.

Wolfman

The copy aide gasped, chuckled and when he'd read the part about testicles and penises, roared with laughter.

"Sure, it's funny," said Ober. "But it put Wolfman right in Chutney's sights. Insubordination. Vicious insults. Union couldn't help. Lateral transfer to night cops. Bye-bye, Wolfie."

"Excuse me," said Bontemps. "May I see that paper?"

"I'll do you one better,'" Ober said, "I'll make you a copy."

Ober answered the phone and said to Bontemps, "Mr. Jones will see you now."

Puzzling over why the paper's ombudsman was acting as a receptionist for the editorial page editor, Bontemps put his copy of the Wolfman letter in his coat pocket unread and entered the office of Mowat Jones, honcho of the Filibuster's editorial page.

chapter IX

LOOPHOLE

M owat Jones, a short, small-boned man with a slight paunch, wore suspenders that pulled his pleated trousers far above his hips. To underlings who disliked him, Jones was known — behind his back, of course — as "High Pockets." A patch atop his head was bald, but the remainder of his head was covered by carefully slicked gray hair.

"Gee whiz, Chester," Mowat Jones said, rising to shake Bontemps' hand and producing a smile through thin lips. "I'm sorry I kept you waiting so long: What can I do for you?"

Bontemps explained his idea briefly: The whole paper was getting behind the city desk's reportage of a crucifixion that, with the proper effort by all departments, could go down as historically significant.

Bontemps wanted to suggest that Jones' role in this grand plan might be to run a lead editorial in tomorrow's paper condemning all these federal executions as inhumanity to man.

"Inhumanity to man. . ." drawled Mowat Jones. His face took on a perplexed look, as if the expression "inhumanity to man" were brand-new to him. "Inhumanity to man. . . hmmmmm."

"Well, in general, that's the idea," said Bontemps. "I realize our operations are supposed to be a hundred percent independent — no influence from city desk on editorial or vice versa. Of course, I realize too that in the past there have been little agreements between the departments." Bontemps hoped he was on firm ground here. He vaguely recalled having heard something about such an arrangement. "But this issue seems just so important, so significant, and this fellow they're going to hang up

— nail up! — to me sounds a notch or two above your ordinary criminal class — "

"Ordinary criminal class," murmured Jones.

"What I mean is that the reader might not find a run-of-the-mill burglar very sympathetic, but this man has some sort of following somewhere in the community — "

"Ordinary criminals or religious lunatics, what the hell difference does it make? Inhumanity is inhumanity, Chester," intoned Jones, using language and inflection he normally rolled out only when writing editorials.

Bontemps sighed with relief. During the long wait for Jones, he'd begun to wonder just what kind of reception he'd get from the master of opinion. Now he could tell they were on a wavelength together. This coverage could be coordinated successfully. He had not overstepped by speaking to the titularly independent editor!

"Yesssss, inhumanity is inhumanity and man is man, and never the twain should meet," said Jones. "But now Chester, I have to caution you: There are distinctions in this business — fine distinctions, but distinctions they nonetheless are, and must be taken into account. Of course, I could go out on a limb and condemn crucifixion per se as a barbarous piece of atavism resurrected by heartless, conscienceless federal bureaucrats. But if I did so, I would most certainly run afoul of an obstacle originating a little closer to home. And by that, I mean Michigan's longtime constitutional prohibition against capital punishment."

"Well, to be truthful," said Bontemps, "I had considered that the state ban on capital punishment would be our chief argument against the practice of crucifixion."

"If we did that," said Jones, "We'd be standing — so to speak — on a trapdoor. Let me explain."

Jones leaned back in his padded leather chair and beamed pleasantly at Bontemps. "Once you begin to unravel the complexities of this, or any other, issue — as we have the time and resources up here to do — you begin to see that many things that at first appeared quite simple are anything but. So it is with crucifixion and Michigan's ban on capital punishment.

"Let us ask the premier, the archetypal, the overarching and commanding question, for everything revolves around it," Jones said. "Does the institution of crucifixion violate Michigan's constitutional prohibition on capital punishment? The answer we find — and believe me, I and my staff of dedicated editorialists have been through and through this one; we have lined entire bookcases with tomes on this issue at no little expense to the Filibuster — the answer we invariably find, Chester, is that No, blast it! No: Our state's fundamental law does *not* forbid the state's taking human life by means of crucifixion.

"Now, you will immediately ask, How did we come to such a conclusion when the Constitution so clearly enunciates its prejudice against capital punishment? Well, Chester, here it is necessary to do what legal scholars do all the time and go beyond what the Constitution actually says — to look at the customs and thoughts actually in force at the time the Constitution was enacted in MDCCCXXXV. At that time, the customary form of judicially terminating a human being's life was to hang him or her by the neck until he or she was quite dead. You see now where I'm coming from? Historically speaking, then, capital punishment in those times boiled down to hanging by the neck. That, then, is all the Michigan Constitution meant to prohibit. A barbarous custom invented by tribal Germans in the Middle Ages, hanging by the neck.

"So you see? You will find no succor in the law's prohibition against capital punishment. Crucifixion is quite legal so long as they don't put a rope around the victim's neck and suspend him by it."

As Bontemps stared at Jones and seconds passed without a comment from the executive editor, Jones filled in the silence: "I'm sorry, it is perfectly legal. Were we to print an editorial defaming crucifixion, first of all, our rival down the street would denounce us for fools who can't read our own state's history, and secondly, publishing the deluge of letters we would most certainly receive from constitutional scholars and attorneys would consume ink enough to bankrupt a financially healthier paper than the Filibuster. So, as distasteful as it may be, we must simply accept crucifixion as a form of execution allowed by the formulators of our state's constitution."

Bontemps was unable to speak. He left Jones' office without even saying good day, thus unintentionally reinforcing his reputation among Filibuster editors as an airhead, an intellectual lightweight who, when confronted with rough-and-tumble political and moral issues, tended to fade into the wainscoting.

Back in the newsroom, he found that reporter Daley Strumm still had not departed for Calvary. Don Strodum was making arrangements for a helicopter to land on the roof of the Filibuster's printing plant and transport the reporter, along with a photographer, to the crucifixion scene.

Rob Wolfman was sitting behind a terminal, reworking a homicide story.

Confused at seeing the chief crucifixion reporter still hanging out in the newsroom, Bontemps mumbled, "When was this thing supposed to get under way at Calvary?"

"About two hours ago," said Wolfman.

"So we're missing it?"

"Have missed it," said Wolfman.

Bontemps' long jaw seemed to become even longer. Somehow, his great plan was coming unglued. What was going on? He looked again at Wolfman and remembered that he had a copy of Wolfman's "vegetarian" memo in his sport coat pocket. He vaguely recalled that the memo had something to do with the transfer of Wolfman from the religion beat — to which he seemed well-suited and well-connected — to night cops.

Well, no time to read that memo now. Wolfman was, after all, the night cops man and somebody else — Daley Strumm — was going to Calvary. Bontemps tried to remember why. Oh, yes, there was nobody else to go. People — he couldn't exactly remember who — were at the big Diversity conference in Honolulu, or they were paid too highly to be insulted with a crucifixion assignment or they had families who would miss them if they were killed at Gethsemane.

Way in the back of Chester's brain there stirred the seed of an idea: Wolfman. Send Wolfman! He had the two essentials of a good reporter: He knew the ropes, and he was expendable. But Bontemps brushed the thought away. He'd just taken a knockdown punch from Mowat Jones, so why risk a knockout slam from Chutney Vipes?

"I've explained it all to Strumm," said Wolfman. "I know one of Jesus' disciples, a kid named John. You don't follow religion and not know John. He's there, at the crucifixion, right now. He's a damned smart young man and keeps great notes. And he's agreed to share them with us."

"God, what a relief. Finally we get a break," said Bontemps. He walked into his office and shut the door.

chapter X

No Checkbook Journalism, But . . .

"S trumm! Daley Strumm!"

Don Strodum's bellow echoed through the long, narrow newsroom and caught the religion writer with his winter coat on, pockets stuffed full of pens and steno pads. Strumm had just pushed the elevator's button, but turned back and faced the assistant city editor.

"Daley, how're you fixed for cash money?"

"I've got $VIII and my MasterCard."

"Not enough. They may not take plastic at Calvary. It's martial law out there. We want you to be able to throw a little largesse around. Of course, as a matter of policy, or ethics, or what-have-you, we don't practice checkbook journalism — you know what that is, don't you?"

"Paying for stories."

"Right. Well, I don't want you getting caught doing that. Emphasis on the *caught*! Ha-ha! But nothing in the Manual of Style says we can't take a few people out for lunch."

Strumm was getting warm with his coat on. He was also becoming more and more nervous as he found a seemingly endless supply of roadblocks to this assignment. Now there was a helicopter on its way to pick him up, and one of his numerous bosses was lecturing him on ethics.

So Strumm said, noncommittally, "It's already past lunchtime."

"Oh, shit, Daley! You know what I mean. Figure of speech. Take 'em out for dinner, a beer, to see the light of the moon, I don't care. Know what? I just thought of this — you can quote me on it: It is a newspaper's duty to print the news and have lunch. How's that for quotable? So break bread with him and what we're hoping is that you'll get an exclusive interview with this Jesus Christ character."

"He's being crucified, Don! What makes you think I'll be able to interview a guy who's been hung from a cross?"

"I don't expect you to do any climbing, don't worry, Daley," Strodum said. "What we're hoping is that the authorities — state troopers — will let him down from the cross long enough to have you run him out for a quick lunch, get his firsthand yarn, then back to Calvary and hammer him back up there on the cross."

Strumm wondered fleetingly if it was possible that this could really be happening in the newsroom of the eighth biggest daily newspaper in the U.S. Take a martyr out to lunch?

"Don," Strumm said helplessly, "He's been up there for two hours already."

"All the more reason to give him a break — half an hour, no more. Believe me, the guy will thank you for it. Wouldn't you give thanks to someone who prolonged your life half an hour? Anyway, don't argue. Chut just had an inspiration. Caninski and Pilate are bosom buddies. Normally, we don't trade on our social connections, at least not so blatantly, but being that we're on deadline — oh, hell, forget all the rationalizing. Leave that for the ombudsman, and just figure it comes down to this: We've got a paper to get out. I'm trying now to reach Caninski by his car phone to see if he'll prevail on Pilate to order those state troopers to let Jesus down for lunch. Now, I want you to go up to the fourth floor to Caninski's office, where the secretaries have an envelope with $CCC in cash for you. Buy somebody lunch, high tea, I don't care. Make sure you spend it all or at least be able to make out an expense form showing how you might have spent it. Now get going, for Chrissake — we've got copy to move!"

Strumm turned and walked briskly to a stairwell. Taking the steps in twos, he made it to the fourth floor in ten seconds, turned and bolted down the hall, wrenching open the plate glass door to the publisher's office.

Wendy, the publisher's white secretary, and Becky, his black secretary, were deep in conversation and paid no attention to Strumm's noisy arrival.

"It has a distinctive, authoritative ring to it," Becky declared.

"I can just hear Dave saying it," said Wendy. "He'd reel it off the top of his head, profound as it is, and make it sound like he just thought of it on the spur of the moment."

"Which he probably did."

Wendy held the framed aphorism at arm's length for both to read:

IT IS A NEWSPAPER'S DUTY TO PRINT THE NEWS, AND RAISE HELL.
— *David Caninski*

"It's so fresh and white, it makes the other one look a little yellow and worn," said Becky as she looked at Caninski's "two bad days" motto.

"It's not by David Caninski," said Strumm.

Both women turned to look at the interloper.

"Excuse me," Strumm murmured. "I'm here to pick up an envelope, er, some money — "

"Who *are* you?" Wendy, the older and more senior of the two secretaries, glared at him.

"Well, I'm Daley Strumm."

"*Who* is Daley Strumm?" asked Wendy.

"I'm the religion writer. I was supposed to come up here."

"Oh, yes," said Wendy, as she relaxed and broke into a big smile.

"Headed out on a big story. We have an envelope for you. There's some money inside that we managed to glean from classified advertising's petty cash. I've got something for you to sign."

"What did you say about Mr. Caninski not having said this?" asked Becky, pointing to the latest motto.

"Well, the raising hell quote isn't from Caninski, although he might have said it."

"He most certainly *did* say it," said Wendy. "I heard him."

"Yes, I understand, but the first person to say it was a man named Wilbur Story, more than a century ago."

"You mean it wasn't original with Mr. Caninski," said Wendy.

"Yes, that's right," said Strumm.

"Please sign here for the money and make sure you account for every penny of it," said Wendy.

Strumm signed the document, slid the bills out of the envelope and into his wallet, and made his way briskly toward the elevator.

Wendy and Becky looked at each other.

"One of us is going to have to tell him," said Wendy. She looked at Becky. Becky looked at her. The two secretaries continued looking at each other wordlessly for quite some time.

Wendy, the white secretary, was thinking that the person best suited to break such an ego-deflating piece of news to the publisher would be Becky. A black secretary would be better qualified for such an odious, indeed risky, task because the boss would be less likely to fire or demote someone whose hiring and promotion so far had earned him a couple thousand buckos in affirmative action bonuses. Caninski had to be told. What he'd done amounted to a flagrant, indeed stupid, case of plagiarism. If it ever leaked to a gossip columnist on the city's other daily, the publisher would look like a colossal ass. And Becky was just the one to tell him. Even should Caninski decide to remove Becky from the office to keep her knowing face from his sight, he would be more likely to promote her to a higher rank and salary, thus earning a further diversity bonus for himself.

Becky looked on the situation rather differently. In her opinion, Wendy clearly was the one to carry the poisoned water to Caninski. First of all, Wendy was white. White bosses didn't stay angry as long at white employees because white bosses didn't have the black flag of skin reminding them of what they'd learned from the crib — that blacks are naturally inferior to whites even when they demonstrate that they're not. Also, Wendy was older, had twenty-one years with the company and had known Caninski long before it became fashionable and profitable to offer jobs to black people. The boss could not be allowed to make a fool of himself in his own office. Somebody had to tell him, and Wendy, obviously, was the one to do it.

Finally, Wendy broke the silence. "I think, don't you, that we really ought to have the old motto reset so its color and typeface match the new one."

Relieved at the implicit suggestion that they keep their mouths shut and do nothing, Becky said, "That is just what I was thinking. I'll take it down to Graphics myself."

So it was that David Caninski's precious saying, "I've never had two bad days in a row," was taken to an area of the paper where, some wags claim, Newtonian laws of physics themselves have been suspended. In the Filibuster's graphics department, the normal rules of good behavior, or what passes for decorum, modesty and decency in a newspaper, had been suspended.

Thus, when Ralph "Denver" Korns was assigned to reset the aphorism, and when he saw to whom it was attributed, the inspiration for a malicious and off-color prank occurred to him.

In tandem with his little trick, three other thoughts quickly crossed his mind: How far will this thing go? Will it be traced back to me? My pension is vested — do I give a shit?

Denver Korns did a very nice job of resetting the Caninski quote. The big Times Roman letters now stood out in dense black contrast to the shiny white paper. He sealed it into a frame and carefully slid the new sign into a large manila envelope, penciled Becky's name on the outside and placed the envelope in a cardboard box meant for interoffice mail pickup.

Smirking, Denver Korns walked back to the graphics department.

This would be his little secret.

I wonder if I'll ever know if I've had any, well, any impact, Korns thought.

chapter XI

THE MEANING OF ASAP

Whenever newsroom pressures bore down hard on Daley Strumm, his actions and his thoughts seemed — to him — to slow down. It was as if he'd suddenly stepped onto the screen of an animated cartoon in which the powers that be — the filmmakers — had deliberately turned down the speed.

So it was with Strumm now as he drove toward the Filibuster's printing plant, searching for the entrance of a sprawling building he had never before been near. There it was — he saw it — a security guard sitting in a concrete-and-glass cubicle between two paved streets. ENTRANCE, the sign on the right said.

Strumm's car lurched to a halt beside the guard post and he jumped out. A woman behind the window slid open a small speaking hole.

"I'm Daley Strumm, I'm a reporter on the Filibuster, and I'm supposed to meet a helicopter on the roof of this plant!" he shouted.

"It's up there," she said, pointing. "Let me see something that shows who you are."

Strumm grabbed at his left back pants pocket, pulled out his wallet, fumbled through a worn plastic ID container and brought forth a ragged piece of Filibuster identification that noted that he was Daley Strumm, age thirty-nine, and belonged to the "ediatoral" (sic) department of the paper.

"Go on in," the guard said with a vague wave.

Strumm jumped back in his car, started it up and headed for the plant parking lot. It was fairly full and getting more so as evening shift printers showed up for work. The Filibuster is a morning paper, so its printing plant begins to come alive late in the afternoon.

He finally found a place to park about a quarter-mile from the big building. Trotting, he arched his neck, trying to catch sight of the chopper on the roof. Though the building was low, it was long, and most of the rooftop was blocked from his view.

Inside the building, he found another security guard. This time, he had his ID ready.

"All the way to the other end of the building for the heliport," he was told. "Then take the elevator to the second floor, get out, look for a staircase opposite the elevator and go all the way up and through the last door and you'll see it parked on a big yellow X."

This time, Strumm sprinted down the hall, slid up to the elevator, punched the UP button and waited.

Back in the newsroom, a frantic scene. Stanley Harrison, graphic arts mogul of the Filibuster, is shouting over a handie talkie.

"You're running out of light! Light!" screamed the graphics chief. Normally, he was too busy writing memos and holding high-level meetings to concern himself with individual assignments, but in this case, there was a helicopter involved. That meant drama and the expenditure of beaucoup buckos, hence a chance to show who was boss in a way that would attract attention across the newsroom.

Atop the Filibuster printing plant, her hair blasted by the downthrust of the helicopter's spinning rotor, Carla Strumpff strained to hear what her boss was saying.

She made out the part about light, but what about it? Maybe the damned fool wanted her to bring the light with her. Those idiots were always asking you to do the physically impossible, thought Strumpff, and then when you did it, they'd laugh when you mentioned a raise.

"Just don't let them go without Strumm," warned Strodum back in the newsroom.

Stanley Harrison pretended not to have heard Strodum.

With the radio jammed tight against his lips, Stanley screamed, "Go! Now! Go! Now!"

It was a simple message that Strumpff couldn't deliberately misconstrue. She nodded at the pilot, who stretched out an arm and helped her into a seat beside him. Carla Strumpff tossed her camera bags on the cramped little jump seat that had been reserved for Strumm.

"Guess we can't wait for Daley any more," Carla said with a smile. She buckled the seat harness. "Maybe this'll teach him the meaning of ASAP."

Seconds later, the chopper lifted off and headed west, toward Calvary Hill. The helicopter gained altitude and turned briefly northward to avoid an incoming jetliner bound for Detroit Metro Airport. To the west, the sun lay hidden behind gray clouds rimmed with brilliant white light.

Atop the Filibuster plant, the roof door burst open and Strumm ran out onto the asphalt. There was the big yellow cross, all right.

The roof was still. There was no sign of a helicopter. Daley Strumm stood staring at the yellow X. Yes, this was the Filibuster printing plant. Yes, this was the plant's roof. Yes, this was even an apparent helicopter landing spot, what with the X, a scattering of charred cigarette butts and, on a wall, a broken fire extinguisher.

Having run through this checklist, Strumm collided with the inevitable question: Where oh where was his helicopter?

If not here, perhaps elsewhere on the roof?

But the rest of the roof, consisting of coarse gray gravel on tar, was fenced off.

This had to be the place.

So where was the chopper?

Strumm felt the despair that sometimes wakened him in the night. He had this recurring nightmare. The situations always varied and usually reflected the story he currently was working on. But the predicament never varied. His basic incompetence as a reporter would be exposed for everyone — most of all for him — to see. Often, the dream had him trying to find the place where he was to meet someone for an interview. Except that he couldn't find the place. He would forget a key part of the directions. He would mistake south for north and hunt in the wrong section of town. For hours, he would search, all the time growing more and more depressed.

Now, here was the nightmare, and it was real. Sent to board a helicopter that everyone said was on a certain roof, he's certain he's found the right roof, but can't find the helicopter.

He didn't wait for the elevator, but ran down the stairs, sprinted back along the corridor and found the security guard.

"Where's the helicopter gone to?" he gasped.

"Why, it's up on the roof," said the guard.

"No — I was up there. It's not there."

"You look real good? It's got to be up there. Where else would it be?" the guard asked.

So Strumm again ran down the hallway, up the stairs and out onto the roof.

No chopper.

He'd have to call the desk.

And say what? That he couldn't find the helicopter the paper had gone to great expense to hire especially for him?

And what if by some strange quirk it was there after all, lurking somewhere around this building? What a fool would he, Daley Strumm, appear to be!

He was losing his mind!

He was getting too old for this line of work. There had to be some detail his memory had failed to grasp. Was he supposed to find the chopper on some other building?

Out of breath, Strumm walked slowly back down the stairs, then along the hall. He didn't speak again to the guard, but walked slowly along the asphalt parking lot to his car, inserted a key in the door, unlocked it, opened the door and slid onto the seat.

How awfully depressing. Daley Strumm felt washed up, dead.

He drove slowly down Fort Street, found an empty parking space and pulled in. He found a pay phone. He was very close to the main Filibuster building, but didn't dare face anyone there.

They'd given him a big assignment, a chance to prove himself on something more than religious thumb-sucker stories, and he'd blown it.

His nightmarish feeling of desolation, of helplessness, powerlessness and incompetence overwhelmed him.

Daley Strumm felt like crying, but he couldn't remember how.

chapter XII

WRITERLY ATTENTION

While Daley Strumm pondered his failings as a reporter on a top-flight metro daily, the Filibuster's fifth floor, home to the features department, was almost too small to contain the joy Minky Maloney was feeling.

Ever since Chutney had called her, all down in the mouth about the nasty memo from Caninski, Minky had brooded about the injustice of it all and wondered how she could help her beloved Chut pull his chestnuts out of the broiler.

Now she had it — a wonderful idea.

The key to rehabilitating Chutney lay in making a proud success of the Filibuster's crucifixion coverage. Chutney simply didn't realize — well, as of yet, nobody at the paper truly realized — how important this story was going to be. Not in the grand terms of history outlined by the megalomaniac Chester Bontemps, but in the more modest success terms required to sustain and advance careers at a major metropolitan newspaper.

In short, it didn't matter what outsiders thought about the Filibuster's coverage of the crucifixion, so long as reporting was perceived, in-house, as hot stuff. And Minky Maloney had the power to condition such perceptions. It was a company publication called "The Write Fluff," a one-page weekly flyer giving cash prizes for the best-written articles in the Filibuster.

Minky Maloney was in sole charge — except, of course, for insertions and deletions by Dave Caninski — of "The Write Fluff," which claimed to be a journal "for prose perfectionists."

Minky hesitated but a second over a trifling debater's point that some critics might raise about what she was planning to do. True, the story wasn't written yet — truth to tell, it wasn't even reported, although the reporter was in a chopper on his way to Calvary right now.

But knowing the people involved, it just *had* to turn out well. Minky was confident that it would. Besides, since when did an editor wait for reporters to confirm their preconceptions before setting a story in stone?

She began writing the lead piece for next week's edition of "The Write Fluff."

Our excellent coverage of the fatal crucifixion of Jesus Christ last Friday — hats off to Daley Strumm and Blaine Monihan — was a nifty demonstration of how a breaking story is enhanced by writerly attention to detail and atmosphere. The vivid excerpts below, the result of on-scene observation by Daley and prose-finishing by Blaine, have nothing to do with such immediately essential information as who was the fanatic crucified, why did he die on the cross, etc. Yet they transported readers, not only to the scene, but to the emotional center of the story, subtly echoing the human truth of what occurred in a way journalism usually abandons to literature. Thus, Daley Strumm and Blaine Monihan share the first prize of $L in coupons to the Pontifex Maximus Grill. Kudos to both of you!

It was a satisfying feeling to know that what had not yet even happened was already etched in the annals of Filibuster newsgathering lore. Now all that was needed was for Daley Strumm to begin filing notes and Blaine — or somebody, for the name could be changed and not damage the article — to do rewrite.

But a thought occurred to Minky. She knew some photographer had been sent to shoot the story. Yes, that egomaniac, Carla Strumpff! It would not do to leave Carla out. Easy enough to write her into the paean. Minky reached for her calculator. What's $L divided by three?

Minky lifted the telephone and dialed Chutney's extension. The phone on Vipes' desk rang and rang and rang.

But Vipes didn't hear it. On another phone he was shouting at Strumm, who was calling in from a pay phone.

"What do you mean, it's gone?" yelled Vipes, incredulous. "Well, where the hell did it go, if you're not on it?"

Vipes slammed the phone down.

"Don! Strodum! What'd I tell you? Goddam, we sent the wrong man to Calvary — this has to be an all-time first."

"What's that?"

"Strumm. Get this. We had that chopper chartered for him, for Strumm alone, and guess what..."

"I give up."

"The bozo missed his flight."

chapter XIII

MAUDLIN IS OKAY

If Don Strodum's replies to his putative boss sounded somewhat curt and peremptory, it is because the weight of the next day's news budget — that list of stories in the making that begins to obsess editors of daily newspapers from the time they wake up in the morning — was beginning to bear down on the deputy city editor.

In addition to the plane crash at City Airport, which would be big news if they knew for sure how many had been killed, there was a long, ragtag list of possible stories that still had to be checked out by reporters. All of this work could have been done much earlier in the day by reporters, had the jobs been assigned promptly. But editors were either at lunch, in meetings or absent in Hawaii.

Just now, the telephone had rung and Rob Wolfman, temporarily back at police headquarters, had announced that the bodies of two women, partially clothed, had been found by some kids beside, but not in, a factory Dumpster.

"Why weren't they *in* the Dumpster?" Strodum demanded.

Whatever reply Wolfman gave apparently was inadequate. "Find out why they weren't in that Dumpster and then get back to me."

There was a pause as Strodum listened impatiently to Wolfman, speaking in a whisper from the police office the Filibuster shared with the Detroit News and Free Press. The NFP reporter was sitting not five feet away from Wolfman, who knew his rival was out of the loop on the Dumpster story because he'd been having a long lunch with a police officer from the Public Information Office whom he was dating. If Wolfman spoke softly, the Filibuster might keep its exclusive.

"Hey, listen, Rob," Strodum cut in, "First of all, find out what those ladies were doing. Were they on their way to temple? If so, it's a big story. But if they were out buying crack cocaine, or something equally illegitimate such as selling pussy, we don't have space for them."

Bodies in — or beside — a Dumpster. That was a run-of-the-mill news story, not the sort of thing the city editor should be involved in. Vipes didn't want to know whatever it was that Rob Wolfman was finding out about. He'd had enough of Wolfman for one day — for one lifetime!

Since his confrontation with Wolfman, Vipes had been out of sorts. Well, to be truthful, his fury dated back a tad earlier, to the surly memo he'd received from the big boss, David Caninski. But it sure was easier to dump blame on Wolfman, the lowly reporter, than to get back at Caninski, the high-and-mighty publisher.

Of course, Vipes still hadn't thought of a way to respond, as he was required, by five post meridian, and the pressure was making him testy. Whatever he wrote would have to be subtly sarcastic, a time-delayed zinger. Oh, he would make Caninski pay, some way. But it would take writerly attention to nuance. Vipes would not want his spite to leap from the page and whack the publisher between the eyes. The chain that owned the august Filibuster also had some tiny papers in the far north reaches of Idaho where recalcitrant reporters and editors could wind up. Next stop, Siberia. Better that revenge lurk in the recesses of Caninski's feverish consciousness, waiting to give him one of those bad days of which he boasted of never having had two in a row.

The very thought of Caninski at this moment frustrated Vipes with a feeling of powerlessness. There was just not much the city editor could do in the way of backstabbing David Caninski. He was impregnable. The man was beloved by corporate upper management, the paper regularly raked in awards for its journalistic swashbuckling, he was a big name in the Imperial Society of Newspaper Publishers — in short, Caninski was golden.

But Rob Wolfman was another matter. Wolfman could be dealt with. And now, Vipes was smarting from Wolfman's unintentional challenge. What more could Vipes do to Wolfman, having already banished him to night cops? Wolfman's perennial insolence was a constant irritant, but today it was definitely the last straw! What more could Chutney do to Wolfman? It was time to find out.

That's why Chutney slipped away from his terminal late that Friday afternoon and left Don Strodum to wrangle with Daley Strumm over missed charter flights. Like the executive editor, Chester Bontemps, Vipes was too busy with matters of consequence to open up his computer file, where the publisher's edict banning crucifixion coverage lay blinking its incessant MSG PENDING signal.

Vipes was headed for Human Resources for some timely advice on the Wolfman problem.

Before he could lay an effective trap of vengeance, though, Vipes had to be sure that Wolfman's behavior really was the straw that broke the camel's back. One thing was sure — Chutney allowed himself a rare grin — one thing Wolfie doesn't know about: There's a stack of evaluations a mile high down there in Human Resources, all about Wolfie, good old Wolfie.

Indeed, it was priceless. By itself, it was an excellent, a superb twist of irony, given Wolfman's self-professed talent for clairvoyance. Wolfman had been overheard in the newsroom boasting that since his last evaluation written by management five years ago, editors had not dared write another one. That evaluation had been a concatenation of barbs that Wolfman had interpreted correctly as a scathing, blistering acid attack aimed at riling him into some stupid action. Vipes understood well that Wolfman had a contractual right to read the piece and that he would exercise that right. So he had crafted — Vipes' word — the evaluation accordingly.

Wolfman had read it, then confronted Vipes with a point-by-point refutation. Wolfman had proven to his own satisfaction that every charge of Vipes' was a contrived lie intended to cover management's shortcomings and outright failures. Or, he had argued, the criticisms were simply scurrilous, malicious slanders, which, if published, would have enabled him to sue the paper for libel. Wolfman had strutted into the Human Resources office, demanded his file, and ostentatiously stapled his response to Vipes' verbal assault.

The evaluations ended.

As far, that is, as Wolfman knew.

What he didn't know was that Vipes had continued writing his annual diatribes, stuffed them in a separate file and then, somehow, forgot to notify Wolfman they were there.

True, this was a violation of state law and the union contract with the Filibuster, but who cares? Unions were in disgrace these days, anyway — completely out of fashion. So Vipes took time to pat himself mentally, spiritually, on the back. All the background work — the file-keeping — would at last pay off. For to severely punish a reporter, which he had a strong mind to do to Wolfman, it is not enough to have one instance of insubordination, as this case of monkeying in the tickler certainly amounted to.

No, some adroit Newspaper Guild attorney might — well, certainly could be depended upon to — argue that historically and as a matter of unwritten policy, the tickler had always been open to all employees — from columnists to copy aides — for contributions of upcoming news events.

Thus, this incident by itself would not topple Mr. Know-It-All-Before-It-Happens, the vegetarian Wolfman. But taken as the latest incident in a long list of trumped-up charges, it might just qualify the night cops man for special retribution. HA-HAH!

Just what form that retribution might take, Vipes was not sure. That's why he wanted to review Wolfman's dossier and consult with a personnel hatchet m— uh, executive — about the, er, possibilities. It would take only a moment, then he could get down to writing his reply to the Caninski rebuke.

Yes, indeed, the straw that broke the camel's back, gloated Vipes. If only Wolfman knew what was in store for him. Vipes delighted in having such control over another person, especially a person who had dared to challenge his newsroom authority.

He spread the file in front of him on a tan Formica table normally used by people taking tests as part of the process of applying for a job at the Filibuster. Vipes had taken such a test here once himself, long ago, but that experience didn't come to his mind now, what with the delight he was feeling at having Wolfman in his grasp.

The file on Wolfman was long — he'd been a Filibuster reporter for twenty-seven years.

Vipes did the arithmetic — yes, that was correct — twenty-seven years of reporting, starting as a copyboy and working his way up. Up! Hah! Up to night cops!

Now to be turned out to graze.

Early retirement was an option, Vipes knew. Not the desirable choice, though. Not ignominious enough.

He read: APTITUDE. . . Hmmm, not too helpful. Wolfman's tests showed a high degree of reportorial aptitude. COPYEDITING SKILLS: Again, superior. GENERAL KNOWLEDGE: Quite high, especially in history, philosophy, religion, literature, mathematics, physics, biology, music and art. Rather low on the sports scale. Hah! Wouldn't you know — Wolfman a sports dumbie.

Wait, here it is — the MMPI. You can always hang 'em with the good old Minnesota Multiphasic Personality Inventory, Vipes had been taught. Yes, indeed, Wolfman has an unusual curve — spikes out on the authority scale. Hates bosses! A congenital rebel.

Whew! Case nearly made. Contempt for management. Plain as day.

Now, it was in here somewhere — yes, Vipes had it: his own clandestine evaluation of an assignment Wolfman had covered years ago. Dionysian fanatics had set off a roadside bomb that killed a truckload of infantry from the XIV Phalanx of Imperial Marines. Vipes read his own typewritten comments.

"Ordered Robert Wolfman, reporter, to proceed to home of family whose son known to be in truck. Deathwatch assignment — Wolfman to observe family for signs of reaction to news re facts about son. Condition of son unknown at time assignment made, but good possibility he's dead. Our best shot at portraying grief of stricken family.

"Receive telephone call from Wolfman. Says he's at pay phone. Filibuster cell phone dead as usual, he claims. Family refuses to allow Wolfman inside home. Claim right to privacy. This writer tells Wolfman privacy insufficient reason for him not to be at family's side during their time of ordeal. As added incentive, I tell him the story is budgeted for Page One. It is four-thirty post meridian. Need story by five if it's to be moved for state edition, which is definite must. Fertile Pulitzer field here.

"Careful instructions to Wolfman: Return to family's home and use charm, force or whatever it takes to get inside. Cash payment ruled out due to no-checkbook-journalism policy, but Chinese carryout okay. This writer suggests Wolfman shoot them the line that we as media have early access to news from official sources coming through wire services plus long-cultivated contacts with law enforcement and military authorities. He can get them word of son's fate before the Marines tell them. Thus, they would benefit from free Filibuster service in their time of travail.

"Wolfman response not entirely audible, although seems to contain words 'drop' and 'dead.'

"Click of phone.

"One hour later, Wolfman calls city desk. He is inside house. Family feels sorry for him standing outside in rain. Pointedly comments that he did not 'buy my way in.' What is meaning? That we were offering money to family? That I, the city editor, had suggested bribery? Gross impudence! A slur if ever was one. Take note: Once again, sarcasm on job by Robert Wolfman not helpful to achieving ultimate editorial goal of paper.

"City desk now knows this family's boy gets a plastic bag. 'Wolfie, they've got a dead centurion there. Do they know?'

"Wolfman: 'No. They still think he's okay.'

"This editor: 'Nix on that. He was one of first bodies pulled. Listen carefully. You sit them down — any other media in there? No? Great! A Filibuster exclusive. Sit them down and break the news. Don't be too gentle. Don't want to make it easy on them. Need reaction. Their son is a goner. Take notes on every tear, every wince, every groan. Watch their faces. If they wring hands, crack knuckles, that is great. Maudlin is okay, but know the limit and phone us ASAP.'

"Wolfman: 'Chutney, you know how to drive, don't you? You got a car, don't you? Okay, you get in that car of yours and drive it out Interstate-XCVI west to Middlebelt, take Middlebelt to Eight Mile, turn left, then right into the trailer park. You come on out here to these people's trailer and you break the news and don't be too gentle, watch their faces, take good notes and phone it all back to the city desk ASAP. I'm not doing your dirty work.'

"Last heard from Wolfman. Classic case of insubordination."

"Well," Vipes said to Peter Osniak, the personnel manager, "what are the possibilities?"

"The possibility was that you could have made a good case for firing him right then. But you can't fire him now for what he did three secret evaluations ago, Chut. If you did, the Guild would take it straight to arbitration, and they'd win. They might have won back then, too. You wanted him to invade that family's privacy, which could be interpreted as a request for a reporter to break the law, or at least put himself in imminent danger of being sued civilly. I know it's ridiculous, but that's the law in this land of ours. No, firing is out. You look disappointed."

"I am. I want to get rid of this guy."

"Well, there may be a better, more subtle way, Chut."

"What's that?"

"Counseling. You can make a case for that. The case of the dead Marine, compounded now by his challenge that you find some new punishment, something worse than night cops. You can make a good case for counseling. The man is obviously under severe emotional stress. The MMPI shows a definite streak of independence, so we can argue he's got an ax to grind with authority in general, and you just got in his way. We can have him in here once a week for therapy. Reporters as a rule are an independent breed. We actually look for that abrasive, anti-authority personality trend, although I wouldn't mention it in this case. Who ever heard of a good reporter who wasn't a maverick? Anyway, they usually go along with counseling for a session or two before realizing the indignity of it all. Then they find a job at some community college, doing PR. You can depend on it."

Weekly counseling sessions, Vipes thought. This might be better than outright firing. Fired, Wolfman would be outside Vipes' control. But in counseling, he would be around as a warning to others of what could happen. He would thus be serving a useful purpose.

"I'm wondering. . ." Vipes said.

"Yes?"

"Any chance I could take part in the therapy sessions — help out with his counseling?"

Pete Osniak chuckled. "If you have the time."

For the first time in days, Vipes felt like the old Chutney Vipes was back. He was elated — all the more so when he returned to the city desk and heard Don Strodum again on the telephone with Rob Wolfman.

"What'd you find out about those ladies' bodies, Wolfie?"

Pause.

"Prostitutes?" Strodum bellowed. He turned to Vipes. "Those two bodies beside the Dumpster were ladies of the night, Chut."

Vipes shook his head.

Into the telephone, Strodum said, "Don't waste your time on whores, Rob — they got what they deserved!"

chapter XIV

NOT AN IDEA MAN, PER SE

Chester Bontemps' office is cushioned from newsroom bumps and whacks by a small anteroom. There, a secretary waylays those reporters and editors so bold as to seek immediate access to the executive editor without the courtesy of an appointment. With his diligent Janus on duty, Bontemps entered his office and shut the big steel door. He shut off his telephone and leaned back against the cold door. In the office of Chester Bontemps, nationally acclaimed editor of the Detroit Filibuster, there was no sign of the newspaper business. An abstract painting by Paul Klee hung from the wall to the left of his desk. On the wall directly opposite his chair hung a collage of family photos, the gift of his mother, which dated back over three generations of Bontempses. Here, with the door shut and the phones off, Chester Bontemps was insulated from the world of daily newspapers. Well, relatively insulated, that is.

For he could not escape, ultimately, from the Filibuster. Bontemps had shut himself up right now because he didn't want any of his people to see the little beads of sweat that had broken out on his brow. It was the same old sweat that always came when things were falling apart for him. And they were falling apart now. He could feel it. What, Bontemps, asked himself, was wrong? The old formula was not working.

The Filibuster was an instrument that would not play for him.

At other papers, where he had been a loudly heralded success, Chester Bontemps' role had been clear: He had acted the part of newsroom cheerleader. He had channeled what he liked to think of as positive energy into the working lives of his people. It was not unusual in the old days for Bontemps to burst forth from the seclusion of his office and hold an impromptu conference — sometimes right on deadline — and pump the troops up with hearty servings of praise.

"You people continue to amaze me," Bontemps would say. "Here we are battling against the combined might of the News and Free Press, and we're practically insolvent, yet you people turn out journalism that is by any standard top-notch, first-rate, par excellence and bar none."

He was not a man of ideas, and knew it. "I'm not an idea man, per se," he would say, and smile.

At other newspapers, Bontemps' lack of originality had worked to his advantage. In terms of climbing a career ladder, original ideas can be a great hindrance. For if you have a good idea, you are obliged to promote or defend it. Conflict is inevitable. You either smack into someone else also upward-bound with a favorite idea that competes with yours for time and resources, or someone tries to steal your patent. So Bontemps' lack of ideas had worked wonders on his own career. It left him free to promote the work of others. That, in turn, made others indebted to him for their career rise. Editors and reporters, emboldened by the brilliance of their own inspirations, would approach him knowing he would not try to beat them with his own thoughts because he had none.

Not that their much-bruited ideas were ever revolutionary. Often they were gleaned from the New Imperial Times Week in Review, or Imperial Public Radio, or Procession magazine. The important thing was that the idea be legitimate — something currently a matter of careful thought and consideration by the nation's most prominent leaders. The secret to success was simply never be ahead of your time. Present the idea to Bontemps, and if it struck him right — and it always did — he'd say, "Wow, guys, great thinking. Sometimes I wonder how we keep quality folks like you at the Filibuster. Why don't the LA Tempo, Philadelphia Inquisition and New Imperial Times just swoop down and hire you all away from me? Whoops! I don't want you getting the WRONG idea now!"

At other places, everybody chuckled at Bontemps' pep rallies and went back inspired. And why not? He'd make sure their stories won some journalism contests. The wonderful thing about newspaper contests was how easily journalists could be gulled into accepting glory in lieu of cash. Where Bontemps came from, they had a saying — "One award is worth three raises."

Get them a sweet national award with a bronze plaque, or even a state or city press club certificate, and they'd shut up about salary raises. Getting his minions their laurels was easy enough, for his lack of originality was generally reflected throughout the corps of journalists at every level. Journalists or their surrogates, the journalism professors, stocked the panels of judges for most awards, and many of these creatures schmoozed at professional conventions.

Unlike the Imperial Symphony Orchestra, say, where prospective instrumentalists auditioned from behind a screen and thus were selected blindly according to ability to perform, journalistic award entries were admitted with their newspapers' and authors' identities emblazoned throughout. Oh, yes! The potential for injustice and favoritism and you-stroke-me-and-I'll-stroke-you was huge.

Awards worked miracles with internal discipline, for they provided simultaneous rewards and punishments for staffers. Want to be nominated for a prize? Then don't behave like a Wolfman, whose name was never mentioned as one deserving of recognition. It was beautifully corrupt, all the more so because nobody dared to say so. And Filibuster people – some of them — were winning awards. Why not? Often, their ideas had been tried so many times before that they had become classics. Paradigms were set. Journalism that didn't conform to the models would be scoffed at. Most likely, though, it would not see print, having been rejected for failure to conform. Journalists never perceived this to be censorship because they were, well, journalists. Winners would be motivated towards ever more obedient behavior, while those who lost, or who were never nominated, would understand that something in them was deficient.

But at the Filibuster, the cheerleading didn't work. Bontemps did no less speechifying. No fewer awards came the paper's way. Maybe the Filibuster was too big. The executive editor felt disconnected from the process. He felt isolated. Oppressed. Chester Bontemps, the honcho who played squash with Herod, the old king, who could trade jokes with Pontius Pilate, felt severely limited in his own office. He felt there were enemies all around, that everything he did was controlled from somewhere else.

Why could he not galvanize this paper into a firm sense of journalistic purpose? Bontemps was stung by the treatment he had received from

Mowat Jones. What was wrong with running an editorial denouncing the cruel practice of crucifixion? More importantly, thought Bontemps, what was so wrong about one editor — and one at nearly the highest level of the paper — suggesting an idea to another editor, who also happened to be located near, though not on, the top rung?

Was some new approach called for? Were the old tricks worn out? Now in his mid-fifties, Bontemps was not prepared to retrain himself. The old ways would have to do. He felt like a boxer whose punches kept bouncing off his rival's head. He didn't know any other way to hit, so he'd keep swinging as he always had.

Fortified with the boxer analogy, Bontemps opened the door of his office and strode with firm resolve into the newsroom. He found Don Strodum laughing at his computer screen.

"How's CROSS?" Bontemps asked, referring to the as-yet-unreported, unwritten crucifixion story's slug, or newsroom title.

"Terrible," said Strodum, who was still chuckling.

"What's so funny?" Bontemps asked.

"Look for yourself," Strodum said. "Beatrice Bird, the new assistant city editor, is editing a story out of the Gethsemane Bureau. Some bozo on the Gethsemane City Council wants the police chief investigated for firing a cop who blabbed about ticket quotas to a reporter. Beatrice, the poor idiot, is trying to improve the story. Here, look for yourself."

Chester bent forward, squinting at the screen. He read:

Councilman Pompeii said, "If they find that everything was according to Hoyle (WHO IS HOYLE? HE IS NOT MENTIONED PREVIOUSLY) and all the rules and procedures were followed, I think I'm going to have some problems with the rules and procedures."

Bontemps stared at the squib for several seconds. Strodum, wishing to have back at his screen, broke the silence. "Birdie doesn't know who Hoyle is. Get it? 'Who is Hoyle? He is not mentioned previously.' That's called an education deficit. Ignorance, in plain English. Somewhere along the line she didn't pick up the basic knowledge necessary to navigate through pop culture. Don't worry, we've copied that one and sent it to everyone in the newsroom. This one is a classic."

The silence lengthened as Bontemps continued staring at the screen, wondering, How is it that this man has time to mock a new, inexperienced editor when we're in the midst of CROSS — a story of enormous significance that apparently I alone recognize?

But he merely said, "Don, I am amazed at your ability to find a tidbit of humor in the newsroom with the pressure of deadline mounting all around you. Carry on."

Bontemps started to walk away, then turned back. A thought had sneaked into his head. A thought! Bontemps had never trained himself in that particular comportment required of those who get ideas, because he so infrequently needed the skill. He didn't know that sometimes it's better to keep your little inspirations to yourself.

"Don," he said, smiling mischievously, "Who IS Hoyle?"

Strodum tried to look puzzled. Of course, he wasn't puzzled at all. He just had to feign befuddlement to cover the snicker that was forcing its way through his brain. Here was the executive editor once again proving what an airhead he was. Didn't know Hoyle.

"Well, it means according to law, according to regulations, Chester."

"Close," said Bontemps. "'Rules of Games.' Rules of Games — good thing to know in our society."

Bontemps moved through the newsroom, watching reporters quietly tapping keyboards in the long, darkened chamber. Strodum had deserved that riposte, yet the satisfaction Bontemps felt quickly vanished. For if Don gave the matter thought, he would realize the executive editor had subtly rebuked him. Lives in a glass house, throws stones, Bontemps thought. That would negate the positive of Bontemps' pat on the back. The old sweat came back on his forehead, and now it trickled from his armpits.

Unbeknownst to Bontemps, Strodum had rolled his eyes and muttered the caustic expression, "Numbskull!" as soon as the boss was out of sight. He began composing a devastating satire on Bontemps that he intended to publish anonymously through the Filibuster's electronic message system. These computerized digs at the executive editor were known as "Chestergrams," and had at times kept industrious reporters and editors busy for hours. Once the hilarity had been so general and long-lived that it caused the presses to start late.

Bontemps looked over his shoulder at his office door, now open. He could not retreat so soon. Bontemps thought of David Caninski. What would Caninski say if he knew about Bontemps' never-ending depression? The publisher's famous maxim, "I've never had two bad days in a row," came to mind. Dave would not allow himself to have such bad moments. It was all a matter of will power, strength of character.

Firmness and resolve, thought Bontemps. Yes, that's the stuff. Mowat Jones may be my equal and thus out of my control, but there are other ways. Yes. Besides, he thought, the editorial against crucifixion wasn't even my idea. Whose idea was it? But Bontemps knew better than to waste energy blaming others. When your merchandise was borrowed ideas, some of them were bound to go sour. When they do, you drop spoiled goods fast, and don't look back.

"There is another piece to this crucifixion story," thought Bontemps. "What is it?"

The word popped into his head so loudly it was almost as if someone had spoken it: graphics.

Aha! Bontemps was in command of the entire fast-growing Filibuster graphics department, which included artists (although they did their work on computer terminals now and not in pen and ink, the title of "artist" was still accorded them), photographers, layout people and hordes of upper-echelon editors to assure that all sorts of careful planning — meetings, committees, lengthy memos — would come unglued, always at press time, to the frustration of everyone except top management, who after all didn't care as long as they saw some pictures in the paper.

Graphics! That was the way to get on top of this story: with art. But as suddenly as the thought — was this another original idea? — crossed his mind, he realized it contained a challenge. He would have to approach Stanley Harrison, commonly known as the graphics czar or art mogul. Or was it Harrison Stanley? Bontemps always had trouble remembering the sequence of people's names when both their names were surnames. A nickname might help, but Harrison Stanley — Stanley Harrison? — was too absolute a monarch of his department to have something as undignified as a nickname. To his face, at least.

Behind his back, he was known as "Harrison Embarrass-us" and

"Stanley Unmanly," strictly out of meanness, poor sportsmanship and a desire to strike back blindly at a man who had power and used it. Of course, such nicknames never made their way up the chain of command to Bontemps' level, so he didn't have the benefit of using one as a mnemonic aid.

Bontemps found a vacant terminal, sat down, and tried to think how to draft a note to Stanley Harrison/Harrison Stanley. The man was known to be very pious. Quite righteous, in fact, and very strict with himself and the people he supervised. Such people always made Bontemps nervous. Complicating matters was the fact that Bontemps hadn't hired Stanley Harrison. Nor had he hired Harrison Stanley. That decision had been made before Bontemps came to the Filibuster. The two were thus — how does the saying go? — not well tuned to each other. Ah, yes, they were not a good fit, that's how it is said nowadays. Their relationship so far had been very formal.

Perhaps, thought Bontemps, it is time to break the ice.

He typed, STANLEYGRAM, and smiled. Hopefully, the graphics muck-a-muck would be amused.

Hey Stan!

Heads up for the Filibuster's eye-catching crucifixion coverage. We want lots of award-winnable photos and juicy artwork for tomorrow's story, which is even now being reported. Let's talk! See you in five.
Chet

That should get his attention, Bontemps thought.

chapter XV

KEYS OF THE KINGDOM

Daley Strumm felt like a shirker. He'd been assigned to a story a long distance away, a helicopter had been booked for him, and he'd botched it. He could not bring himself to speak to anyone at the Filibuster right now. He could imagine what they were saying about him back in the newsroom.

Religion writers got little enough respect as it was. They were believed to be less than competent at ordinary cops-and-robbers reporting. Half a notch above the music critic. But to miss his ride! To fail before he'd even started the assignment. Well, Daley Strumm knew disgrace, and this was it.

He entered the tall old Gothic building by the rear door, and slunk down the hallway in dread that he'd encounter someone from the newsroom. He decided not to use the elevator because that was the chief meeting ground at the paper. Instead, he walked up the stairs. Engrossed in his morbid, self-incriminating thoughts, he didn't notice when he got to the third floor, and kept hiking up past the newsroom. At the fourth floor, he pushed open the big wood-and-glass door and walked out onto hardwood. He felt vaguely disoriented. He knew immediately that this was not the third floor because there was no darkened newsroom to confront him.

Directly in front of him, standing at the bank of elevators, he saw Rob Wolfman and Melanie Munch, the restaurant critic.

Melanie held a tray of pastries. Honey-saturated baklava, candied croissants, little cigar-like rolls covered with green frosting. "I couldn't get Photo out there to take the picture," Melanie was saying. "It was like Dearborn was too far, or something."

"Dearborn doesn't exist for Photo," said Wolfman.

"Well, I put the assignment through three times, Rob. The first time, they said they never saw it. I sent it down again, made an appointment for two o'clock. Photo confirmed, then called the baker at two, right when they supposedly were to be there. They said they weren't coming. No reason, just flat not coming after the guy baked all this stuff and set it up nice and pretty. So I sent it down a third time. They didn't even bother to call. Just didn't show. So I hit on this idea."

"What's that?" said Wolfman.

"Well, Rob, there's an old saying in the newspaper business: If you can't get Photo to come to the picture, bring the picture to Photo. Look — aren't these just the most exquisite Middle Eastern pastries you've ever seen? Mouthwatering? Ha-ha! Hands off, Rob, my lad. You can have some later, after the picture."

"They'll be pretty stale by then, Melanie. Hey!" Rob Wolfman had caught sight of a slinking Daley Strumm. "Daley! It can't be you — you're at Calvary."

Strumm, his back to Wolfman, halted. He would have to face the music sometime. He turned, hangdog, and mumbled something garbled, ending in "bad luck."

"Luck has nothing to do with it," Wolfman said. "Bad planning is what it is. If those yo-yos that run this paper had any brains, they'd have sent a team of reporters out to Calvary a week ago. This is the story of a lifetime. The story of all time, Daley."

"Looks like I'll never cover it."

"'Cover'? You'll be a witness, Daley. You're witnessing, not reporting. There's a reason why all this stuff is happening. Huh! Maybe there's a reason for all this poor planning at the Filibuster. Maybe this story isn't supposed to be covered as news."

"It's not going to be."

"Okay, let me guess what happened — the city desk chartered a helicopter and before you could get on, Photo commandeered it and took off. Right?"

"All I know is that it was not there where it was supposed to be. You think Photo went without me?"

"I know about these things, Daley. And you're pretty discouraged, pretty down in the mouth what with all the blaming of yourself, right?"

"Well, wouldn't you be?" said Strumm. "What kind of measure of competence is that, to miss your ride?"

"No measure at all if the chopper is hijacked. You want to hear how the rest of your assignment will go?"

"No!"

"Let me tell you anyway. First, despite what you're thinking, Chutney will not chew you out for missing the whirlybird. He'll tell you to find a company car and drive to the Gethsemane Bureau."

"No! I don't want to hear it!"

Strumm had sworn after the last time that he wouldn't listen to any more of Rob Wolfman's prophecies. That time, he'd been writing furiously on an article about Detroit's High Priest Shoktrup when Wolfman started reeling off what he claimed was about to happen. It had seemed absurd. Strumm's story was slotted for page one and he had three editors breathing down his neck to get it finished.

"I told you then what would happen," Wolfman recalled. "You listened and laughed. I said they'd take you off that Shoktrup story and send you out to cover the First Lady's plane landing at Metro Airport. I said you'd hustle and arrange an exclusive interview with the First Lady, but that when you called to announce your triumph to Vipes he'd wave you off the story and send you to a supposedly big explosion in the burbs. When you got there, I said, you'd find out it wasn't a big explosion, and it was in a poor man's trailer park, not a ritzy condo complex.

"Nonetheless, I predicted that, good reporter that you are, you would interview the mayor, the fire chief, the police chief, three firefighters and several people whose mobile homes were gutted by flames, smoke and water. When you found a pay phone — because the Filibuster cell phone wouldn't connect — there would be a line of reporters waiting to use it. None of their cells worked, either. In that line would be Blaine Monihan, despite his alleged two thousand-bucko-a-week salary. Blaine would also have interviewed the mayor, the fire chief, the police chief, three firefighters and several victims. As the pair of you cursed the editors for double-teaming the assignment, Peg Morris would appear, having interviewed the mayor, the fire chief, the police chief, three firefighters and a swarm of victims. When the three of you phoned in, the desk would cancel the story because it wasn't ritzy condos that blew up. And then the next day, when you opened up the News and Free Press, lo and behold, the other paper's reporter cashed in on the exclusive interview you set up with the First Lady — and you got chewed out for missing that story. Was I right on all counts?"

"You were right — which is why I don't want to hear your prophecy today, Rob. I don't want to know what shit the future holds for me."

"Okay, I'll shut up. But just one word of advice: If you come across a man called Peter, tape-record what he says. Please?"

"Well — "

"Listen, let me tell you about yourself. . . why you were chosen for this assignment."

"I think it was because Chutney thought the paper could get along without me in case I got killed."

"It's true that's why Vipes and Strodum think they picked you instead of the factotum Caesar O'Toole. But that's not really why you were picked. Because you weren't really picked by Strodum and Vipes. You were selected by a higher power. The person who witnesses this story must be someone who is not a real newspaperman."

Strumm flinched, pulling back in anger.

"Don't get defensive. I know you've worked hard to prove you can do the same things real reporters do. But let's look at you. Daley Strumm never went to journalism school. He never sat through a journalism class in his life. He secretly laughs at the people who wasted their time in that fashionable pursuit. He knows that academic journalists are has-beens or wannabes whose only real professional knowledge is a how-to primer on sucking up to managers in the big career enhancement race.

"Daley Strumm's father teaches medieval history. His mother is a linguist. The result is that Daley Strumm is a scholar. He went to college and studied English and French and German and lots of history. He wrote short stories that were witty and polished. He wrote a master's thesis on the genesis of Chaucer's *Canterbury Tales* in certain tavern yarns current in the High Middle Ages. Daley Strumm is an artist and a scholar.

"But art and scholarship don't mix with newspapering. They are mutually exclusive callings, Daley. Except for right now. On this particular occasion, the story calls for something more than a career-striving, byline-poaching egomaniac news jockey. The job description this time is to observe the death of Our Lord."

"Listen, Rob, I'm always interested in your ideas, but right now I've got to make myself known once more at the City Desk, and I'm not yet steeled for the task."

"You don't need to be steeled for it. They won't send anyone else because you're the only one who's in the cards. Sometimes history needs imbeciles, and never before were morons so badly needed as now at the Filibuster to assure that you and only you make this trip. Of all the times for the Society of Amalgamated Minority Journalists to pick for a unified Diversity cluster-fuck, why do you think they held it this weekend? It was not their decision! The plain fact is that if one underaged, dark-skinned and preferably female intern were convenient to give Chester or Chut a five-grand bonus boost, do you think you'd be going to Calvary? For once, that old white guy target on your back is doing some good. Now, just go down and tell Chutney to give you a Filibuster car so you can get to the story.

"And one thing — "

"What?"

"Please take a tape recorder."

"Strumm!" On his way for a private moment with Minky Maloney, Vipes had spotted Wolfman and Strumm. He was still feeling upbeat, and where the sight of Wolfman once would have driven him into an angry funk, now he was reminded of the joyful times he would soon be having in the therapy sessions he would soon be guiding the night cops man through.

"Jesus H. Christ — " Vipes stopped, wondering where he'd picked up that expression. No matter. "Daley, what are you doing here? We need you at Calvary! Oh, yes, I remember: Photo ripped off the chopper. Well, just another one of those unforeseen Filibuster fuckups. Sometimes I wonder how we put out a paper, what with some folks tending to more than their assigned jobs, Wolfie. Tell you what, Daley, there's a company car with your name on it down in the Filibuster lot. I was holding it for Mink — Oh, well, not important. Keys are in it. Take it and get going. Oh, wait a minute — here, take this Filibuster cell phone. Call us just as soon as you get to Gethsemane, okay?"

Vipes handed his company cell phone to Strumm.

From a few yards down the hall, several voices shouted, "Chutney!"

"Hey, Chut!"

"Join us!"

It was a swarm of photographers, men looking uncomfortable in limp knit ties, women in stiff white blouses. Several had cameras dangling from straps hung on shoulders or around necks.

An old man sitting behind a metal desk was repeating, "They're here to have their picture taken. Leave them alone! They're here to be photographed."

"Don't be such a drip, Sweeney!"

A man who was not encumbered with a camera picked up a tray of delicious-looking Lebanese pastries and passed them around the group.

"Good old Melanie Munch — ha-ha — ain't *much* at writing, but she shore do know how to cook!"

"Thanks, don't mind if I do," said Vipes, and helped himself to four pieces of baklava.

Three for me, thought Vipes, and one for the Mink.

chapter XVI

A PICTURE MAN

In his office a few yards from where his photographers were rapidly
devouring Melanie Munch's photo opportunity, Harrison Stanley —
that was his name, not Stanley Harrison — was a very frustrated fellow.
He was a sandy-haired man with smooth cheeks, piercing black eyes
and a small, narrow-boned frame. He stood beside his desk, alongside
which he had been pacing in short strides. He was about to begin pacing
again, a habit he fell into when things were going somebody else's way
and not his.

For Stanley Harrison — sorry, Harrison Stanley — was embroiled
in a project right now that he felt was, well, beneath his dignity. He was
setting the record straight about himself, a chore he felt quite honestly he
should not ever have been asked to do.

If Chester Bontemps had appeared outside Harrison Stanley's office
at precisely this minute, he would have heard a long, high-pitched howl.
Stanley was not aware that he made this noise, but everyone who worked
near him had become accustomed to hearing his long, extended groans.
It was a drawn-out drone, an expression of combined irritation, frustration, fury.

"When am I going to get this blamed Q & A done?" he moaned.

Stanley did not swear, but substituted words like "blamed" and
"darned" and "gollywhomping" for harsher language.

The Q & A was a question-and-answer-page planned for an upcoming issue of the Filibuster's in-house magazine, "Pardners." The Q &
A was David Caninski's idea of an ointment he hoped to plaster over

the pus of discontent growing in Stanley's graphics department, chiefly among — wouldn't you know? — photographers and artists.

The problem: Harrison Stanley was being systematically and maliciously misunderstood. A view of Stanley was being propagated that depicted a thirty-two-year-old power-hungry monomaniac and religious zealot who had driven the best photographers to quit while others less brilliant malingered on, poisoning the working atmosphere with their bitterness. There was a perception afloat that Stanley had surrounded himself with young, ambitious bootlickers. Complaints about Stanley had made their way to Caninski, who had hired the graphics czar to be a graphics czar and force some discipline on the uncontrolled monkeys and self-proclaimed egomaniac artistes who had for decades ruled supreme in the photo department.

In fact, Harrison Stanley was just what the publisher needed: a closet nazi with a will of steel, a self-righteous and unswerving conviction that whatever he did was right and whoever opposed him was the devil incarnate. But no way would it do for people to have too clear a view either of Caninski's purpose or Stanley's true nature. Hence, the Q & A, meant to plaster over the misconceptions through the public relations smoke machine known as "Pardners."

But the idea did not please Harrison Stanley. "If they don't know who or what I am, let them find out the hard way!" thought Stanley.

That was not something you said to David Caninski, however. To David Caninski you said, "Fine. Excellent idea, the time is ripe, etc. But I have just one stipulation — that I be allowed not only to answer the questions, but to pose them."

This suggestion caused David Caninski to hesitate for a few seconds out of courtesy to the vague metaphysic known as journalistic ethics. Or perhaps it was simply out of concern for a practical matter, to wit, that Leo Ober, the ombudsman, had already been asked to interview the graphics king and had his list of questions in hand.

To shunt Ober aside would cause temporary embarrassment and give the appearance that the Q & A was rigged, a sham, a parody of good journalism.

"Look, Dave," Stanley had argued, "as long as this whole thing is contrived — I'm going to know the questions before they're asked in any case, and our purpose is to mold employee opinion, not inform, and you said I could edit the whole thing before publication — so why bother with the sham of having Leo interview me? Cut out the middleman! I'll just write the whole consarned thing — think up the Q's and A's myself! Hee-hee! Then, if you want to give it respectability, simply slap Ober's byline and mug on top of it."

David Caninski knew that the back-of-the-newsroom crowd, the grumblers and lily-livered whiners among the photography and reportorial staff, would find this setup shocking. They would probably call it a fraud or something even worse — unethical. But David Caninski had been called a fraud before by these same detractors. The spiters had not retarded the rise of his career. Besides, if this arrangement made his graphics man happy, fine. The chronic bellyachers would always find something to gripe about. If it happened that one of their complaints was legitimate, who cared?

He knew one thing for sure: Ober wouldn't dare complain. He'd already been demoted from the powerful position of news editor to the conspicuous but insignificant position of ombudsman, and now spent his workday answering reader complaints and writing weekly columns about newspaper morality that nobody read.

Now, though, Stanley was regretting his move. He'd gotten his way, only to realize suddenly that he had to finish this tomfool Q & A before the end of the day. It was not going well. He was, after all, a picture man, not a word man.

He moved with sudden, jerky motions to his desk. That was great! A picture man, not a word man! Wow! Good stuff. Use it in the Q & A, somehow. Now, what was the question?

Q: How do you manage to obtain such unflagging inspiration from your photographic staff?

Stanley thought about that. He had to be careful not to step too closely toward the truth here. First, he wasn't sure he'd describe what he was obtaining from those hyenas as "unflagging inspiration." Dumb obedience was what he wanted, and was beginning to receive. But to the public — in this case, the narrow public consisting of the two thousand or so Filibuster employees — "inspiration" was the image he wanted to plant. So far as inspiration could be quantified through awards, it was there, abundantly there. Stanley made sure the journalism contest judges were swamped with entries. He even judged a few of the contests himself, and was friends — he made sure of this — with many of the other judges; he paid for a few of their lunches so they couldn't help having warm and fuzzy thoughts about the Filibuster. Could they? Anyway, every possible photo competition had its Filibuster contestants, so, naturally, there were, thanks to the law of averages, some winners.

That didn't mean there were no problems. Stanley had been on the job only six months, but he knew morale was terrible in his department. He had moved quickly to do something about the floundering esprit. First, he had issued a dress code. One sign of poor morale was the sloppy way his photogs were dressing. Blue jeans, sweaters. Not one of the men wore a tie, not one of the women seemed to own a skirt or a dress. So Harrison Stanley declared ties and coats mandatory for men, skirts and blouses with nylons and flats — he was willing to bend on the matter of high heels — de rigueur for women.

"I'm not being mean," he said in a memo. "I want you folks to think better of yourselves."

There were many who resisted his dress code, of course. First, the bellyachers — chiefly old-timers — complained that, given the unpredictable nature of their jobs, they needed to be dressed for emergencies. One minute you're shooting Caesar Augustus himself, next minute it's an oil spill on the beach of Lake Erie. You don't want to ruin good clothes at a plane wreck, train derailment, etc.

Stanley listened to that argument and met it characteristically, by ignoring it. Thwarted, the grumblers turned to guerilla warfare. Together with complicated explanations about workplace-related damage, expense vouchers started appearing — claims for reimbursement for ruined suits, shoes, pants, overcoats.

Stanley had expected the escalation and was ready for it with a custom-made rubber stamp — a big black square, and inside the square, in block letters: REFUSED.

One day an expense voucher came through from Sweeney Fletcher, the worst of the curmudgeons. Fletcher was the oldest shooter on the staff. He had been at Pearl Harbor on December VII, MCMXLI and shot pictures of Japanese torpedo bombers coming at his battleship. Through the attack, Sweeney shot frame after frame.

Stanley had heard the story, although not from Fletcher, who was tired of telling it. It was a tale that annoyed Stanley. Just because Fletcher had been on a boat and gotten bombed, everyone was in awe of him. It was stupid, knee-jerk patriotism. How was a younger man who had a high draft lottery number during the Vietnam War going to compete with a record like that?

Subconsciously, Harrison Stanley also resented Fletcher's name. Or rather, names. Like Harrison Stanley, both of Sweeney Fletcher's names were surnames. As if the graphics department had two heads! It was no secret that within the Filibuster there was widespread admiration and love for Fletcher. Stanley had no choice, then. Fletcher must be encouraged. Encouraged, that is, to leave the Filibuster. You can't have two graphics moguls.

Thus, Harrison Stanley welcomed Sweeney Fletcher's expense voucher. He read the photog's demand for reimbursement — for a hat lost on assignment — as a direct challenge to his authority. So Stanley deducted the $XX cost of the hat from Sweeney's expense check and, so Sweeney would not miss the point, he photocopied the voucher, with his comment scrawled across it: "The Filibuster does not pay for lost, damaged or stolen personal items. HS"

The following week, Stanley received another expense voucher from Fletcher. It was a lengthy, itemized list of out-of-town expenses at a Herod University football game, but no mention of a hat.

At the bottom of the voucher, Sweeney had written, "The hat's in there, HS. You find it. SF"

The move took Stanley by surprise, but he chuckled anyway. "The hat's in there" was an old line. Unlike Fletcher at Pearl Harbor, Stanley was prepared for a sneak attack. He didn't know where it would come from, or who would deliver it, but the retaliatory strike was ready.

First, Sweeney would be paid for the entire expense voucher as he had turned it in, not excluding the hat.

Second, Stanley — with Dave Caninski's approval — sent the following news item to the in-house propaganda vehicle, PARDNERS.

A general expansion throughout the graphics department enables us to fill a long-empty position in the photography department — that of an obit photo editor. Because of his long experience with the people of Detroit, especially with those at an advanced age where they will soon be gracing our obit pages, veteran Filibuster shooter Sweeney Fletcher has been chosen to hold this new title. Anyone interested in applying for the general assignment photographer vacancy left by this promotion should contact Harrison Stanley. HS.

What this "promotion" meant for Sweeney Fletcher was giving up his cameras, motor-drives and heterodox assortment of lenses, along with the rush to be first at the scene of a major car wreck, homicide or plane crash. Now, Fletcher would spend his time calling funeral homes and beseeching morticians for photos of dead people. No more out-of-town football games. It was a promotion with no raise and a metal desk at the entrance to the photo department.

Stanley liked to think of Fletcher as a living monument to the new czar's power. The fate of the old Navy vet got the point across better than a thousand memos. So did Stanley's policy of placing young, inexperienced and preferably minority people on the fast track and promoting their work, giving them raises, while letting the older hands — no matter their race and gender — eat their dust. And if the young people got some experience — it's amazing how even young people catch on fast! — there was always the example of Sarah Bukari out in Siberia, excuse me, the Gethsemane Bureau. It's really easier to deal with those minority people — especially the blacks — who don't play ball. The higher you lift them, the farther they fall.

So that was the way it really was. But how to answer the question?

A: You don't inspire photographers any differently than you inspire anyone else. Our staff is made up of highly talented — indeed, brilliant — people who know how to pull together in the clutch. The best inspiration is the desire to do the best job they can.

Q: Could you tell us how photographers and reporters — sometimes thought of as an oil-and-water mixture — are able to collaborate at the Filibuster?

A: Planning. No other way. Planning is the key to doing a job well.

Q: What about the oft-heard criticism nowadays that the writing — the reporting — is playing second fiddle to the pictures, that stories are made or broken by the quality of art that they generate?

A: Hogwash. Baloney. Just blamed poppycock. Not worth a retort.

Stanley H — I mean Harrison Stanley — paced rapidly now, back and forth alongside his desk as he dictated questions and answers breathlessly into a tape recorder. Ping. He stopped suddenly. What was that soft, fluttery metallic noise receding underneath his desk? Could it be? Out of the corner of his eye he'd seen something copper-colored, disk-like, just for an instant before it vanished under his desk.

"Oh no!" he screamed. "Not another one!"

So it was that when Chester Bontemps stepped into Harrison Stanley's office, he did not at first see the graphics czar. He saw a metal desk with a glass top covering a large calendar. A green writing terminal sat beside the empty chair. The screen was blinking its incessant MSG PENDING — probably, Bontemps thought, to announce his note. Apparently, Harrison had not read the memo and didn't know Bontemps was coming for a visit.

Then he saw Stanley. Rather, he saw the graphics boss' feet waggling an inch above the floor. The rest of what presumably was Stanley's body was invisible, prone underneath his desk. His feet gave little jerks as Stanley tried to worm his way under the desk.

Chester Bontemps was embarrassed for the man. It was so unexpected. He didn't know Stanley well, but he'd been impressed with the man's aura of propriety and dignity.

"Harry," Chester said. He was unsure whether "Harry" was a proper nickname, or even whether he was making a colossal blunder in not calling him "Stan."

But the man needed to be notified that his boss was present.

At the sound of a voice, the feet began backing and jerking outward. Eventually, the thin young man raised himself to turn and stand before his boss. He rubbed dust balls from the elbows of his Harris tweed sport coat.

"I suppose you weren't able to see my memo," said Bontemps, trying to be tactful.

"Memo?" said Harrison in a high, nervous, squeaky voice. He glanced distractedly toward the bottom of his desk.

"I sent it by electronic mail."

"Oh! Hee-hee! Chester, I rarely look at that terminal. Suppose I should, but you know. . ." He paused as an idea suddenly popped into his head. It had been lying there, waiting its turn. "I'm a picture man, Chester, not a words man. Graphics is the name of my game. So, what can I do for you?"

"Well, graphics is the game we're currently playing. We need to plan for the big push we're making on the crucifixion story."

"Crucifixion," Stanley said absently. Again he glanced anxiously at the floor under his desk. "Crucifixion."

"It's on the budget for tomorrow's paper," Bontemps said. "Carla Strumpff is on her way out there by helicopter."

"I vaguely recall — "

"Your people in the newsroom know all about it. They ordered the chopper to take off without our reporter."

"Good, good. There's no need of a reporter."

"Well, actually, I thought there was. He's finding another way out there."

"Well, golly, Chester, I'm sure they sent her on for good cause. Was your man late? Your reporters do have a way of being late. That relaxed attitude can cost this newspaper in terms of wasted time and lost story opportunities. I've nearly eliminated that kind of systemic inefficiency from my department and would be glad to counsel you anytime you desire to wipe it out of the newsroom. It's mainly a matter of changing attitudes to change behavior. My formula is simple: Mix punishment with reward and never let your employees know when they can expect either."

"Yes, Harrison, well, that's not why I'm here. I need your cooperation for an all-out effort to be number one in our portrayal of this crucifixion."

"Who's the crucifee?" Stanley blinked, turned his head, sneaked a look at the floor beside his desk, as if something underneath were about to hop out, escape.

"What?" said Bontemps. "'Crucifee'?"

"Chester, the story, artwise, boils down to one of crucifees and crucifiers. That's what we photograph. Anything else is a sideshow."

"Yes, well, our religion writer, Daley Strumm, is on the way with instructions to get as close to one of the victims as he can."

"'Victims'? I assume the crucifees are being punished? Have committed crimes?"

"According to Pontius Pilate — "

"Well, then, I would hardly term them victims. They are getting their just deserts. Nonetheless, if there is some situation of anguish to be photographed, I suppose we could oblige. However, might I ask a question or two?"

"Shoot."

"Why, first of all, have you sent a religion writer to cover this crucifixion?"

"Well, because. . . " Bontemps hesitated. He recalled hearing something about Strumm being expendable, but decided to use a superficially more compelling explanation. "Strumm is the religion writer, and this is a religious crucifixion. The chief victim is known by his followers as the Messiah, and they think he fulfills a prophecy that the son of God will come to teach the people of Earth."

"Okay, that answers my first question. Now, might I return to my previous point: Why have you sent a reporter at all?"

"Why, to talk to people at the scene, to get the story and then to tell it."

"Don't you think this story could be told better with pictures?"

"I was thinking of pictures and reporting."

Stanley shook his head, frustrated. "Chester, if you only knew how hard it is to implant new ideas! With very few words and a lot of big color pictures, we could tell the whole world about this Messiah. But if you let a deskbound intellectual like Daley Strumm at this thing, he'll analyze and paraphrase and yarnize it to death.

"Now, I don't really mind that he's there — he may be able to assist our photographer with some legwork. But think, man, think down the road. Not just for tomorrow's paper, but let your mind roam through the possibilities. With the proper promotion, we could publish our own Filibuster book on crucifixion. There's a potential gold mine there, but that takes photos — lots of them. We can have our artists render beautiful four-color graphics of crucifixions past, present and future. Schematic diagrams. How does it work? What are the mechanics? The evolution of the cross. Who are the most famous crucifiers, crucifees? Maybe there's a crossword puzzle in it. Hee-hee — get it? *Cross*word. Most certainly we put our editorial cartoonist onto a series of lampoons. Maybe there's a separate book of cartoons.

"You see the possibilities? Leave it to me, Chester. But lay off the reporting — it complicates the story."

Chester Bontemps, numb, allowed a stiffly grinning Harrison Stanley to pump his hand, then watched as Stanley knelt beside his desk and began crawling underneath.

What, Bontemps wondered, is the graphics czar's fascination with the underside of this desk? Maybe a little humor would help.

"Is there a meeting under there?" asked Bontemps.

Harrison Stanley's voice came up, muffled: "Lost a penny."

chapter XVII

COMMON TOUCH

Had Daley Strumm listened to the clairvoyant Rob Wolfman's detailed prediction of what was in store for the Filibuster's crucifixion reportage, he might have preceded his attempt at driving out to Calvary with a hike to the nearest full-service gas station. There, he would undoubtedly have used his credit card to buy a twelve-volt car battery. That way, the trials he suffered in the Filibuster parking lot, while certainly not eliminated, would have been measurably less severe.

Daley Strumm sat behind the wheel of a red station wagon which had "Detroit Filibuster" emblazoned in Gothic print on both front doors.

He turned the key, and nothing happened. He tried it again. Again. Again. Finally, he searched under the dashboard until he found the lever that unlocked the hood. He pulled it, and the car made its first noise, a soft CHUNK of metal letting go its grip on metal.

Strumm hopped out of the station wagon, opened the hood and peered at the engine. Along the side of the engine well on its own little platform rested a battery. At least it had not been stolen or cannibalized for another Filibuster car. So that was the battery. Now what? What good was looking at it going to do?

Strumm stuck his head back inside the car, inspected the floor, front and back. No jumper cables.

Slowly, the religion writer sank onto the seat. His hand rose to his forehead, thumb and forefinger kneading his brow. Idly, he wondered if this was really happening. Or was it a dream? First, he's yanked off his regular story to cover a cops item. A gruesome execution. Then he misses the helicopter. Now this. Assigned a car that won't run. What more could go wrong?

Fleetingly, it occurred to him that this might be a test. Was this whole fiasco carefully designed to find out if he had what managers at the Filibuster liked to call "the write stuff"? Were all these screwups just Vipes' sadistic way of toying with him prior to announcing that the august, scholarly religion writer was taking the fall? It was a safe bet that Strumm wasn't going to pass this test and would wind up running the day cops show over at Detroit police headquarters. A junior version of Rob Wolfman, holding down a corner of newspaper purgatory.

The thought of Vipes' possible sadism had a galvanizing effect on Strumm. He got angry and smacked his head on the roof of the car as he exited. He'd forgotten that he was seated in a small station wagon and not in his steel swivel chair back in the newsroom.

He got out of the car and looked at the other vehicles in the lot. There were perhaps fifteen or twenty cars here, belonging to Filibuster staffers or to the paper itself. Strumm walked slowly in and out between the cars, hoping to see jumper cables. But it was spring; most people had retired their cables to the basement or garage. Besides, these cars were all locked.

In his pocket, he carried the city editor's cell phone, but he was not used to having his own portable phone and it didn't occur to him that he could simply call the Filibuster newsroom from where he stood. Instead, Strumm walked over to the small guardhouse. He could see through the large window that there was nobody inside. Nobody to help him. He stepped inside, lifted the telephone handset and dialed the city desk number. It rang perhaps ten times before Strumm began counting. He let it ring twenty times, thirty times, forty times. No answer. Perhaps he'd dialed a wrong number. He hung up, dialed again.

Now if that city desk phone had been placed near the bar at the Honolulu Hilton Hotel, it would have been snapped off its cradle by an alert bartender who would have called out, "Is there anyone from the Detroit Filibuster here?"

A dozen half-crocked editors, reporters, photographers and other flotsam from the Filibuster would have fought to be first responders to Strumm's call.

Twice that many Filibuster staffers were off-duty, but collecting regular pay while attending — expenses covered by the Filibuster — various workshops and seminars on minority employment issues. To those who were not there to experience what must have been incredibly joyous experiences of cross-ethnic bonding, it's not clear from the bar bill exactly what lessons were learned.

Understandably, some current Filibuster staffers were being lured to other papers with promises of higher salaries and more conventions, but by the same token, Filibuster recruiter Mort Morton was hard at work simultaneously trying to retain those threatening ship jumpers with even bigger promises of salaries and far more conventions. At the same time, he was doing his best to entice current staffers from any other paper or anyone of presumed ethnicity from any provenance, be it probation officer, taxi driver or ex-convict, to sign on as highly paid reporters — no experience necessary! — with the Filibuster.

"Hey," said one Filibusterer, laughing, "what happens in the year MMXXI, or whenever whites are themselves a minority? Do we invite them to our Unity convention?"

That one brought down the house.

Meanwhile, back at the Filibuster, at fifty rings — five minutes of waiting — there still was no answer. Strumm was not often outside working a breaking story, or he would have known this was not so easily blamed on the Unity convention. It was just one of those times when nobody was willing to pick up the phone.

Daley Strumm read more into it. He began to wonder: Is this being done on purpose to me? He walked back to the car. Incredible! Not even on the road, and the crucifixion was more than likely over.

We should perhaps note a curious aspect of Strumm's attitude toward this assignment. That is, he viewed it as something akin to an athletic event. He'd never covered an execution. It had never even idly occurred to him that someday he might, as a news reporter, be called upon to watch another human being suffer deliberately inflicted death contrived by the minds, hearts and hands of his fellow man. To Strumm, at this point in the assignment, getting to the crucifixion was more important in his mind than the event itself, which remained an abstraction. A word.

"Crucify."

How many times had he used that word lightly, to connote some-body's offhanded claim of being persecuted?

What did it really mean?

Daley Strumm wasn't thinking about that now. Plenty of time to think — or at least to improvise that facsimile of thought which news-papers like to plug under the subheading of "analysis" — when he got to Calvary.

There was, Strumm knew, a gas station four blocks from the Fili-buster building. Four city blocks. He could see no other way. He ad-justed the wagon's gear lever to the neutral position, opened the driver's-side door, kept his right hand on the steering wheel and leaned his left shoulder against the door. He pushed. The car budged. He let go. The car rolled back. He pushed. It rolled. He leaned harder. It rolled faster, then slowed.

By this means, Strumm forced the wagon to the end of the parking lot drive and let it stop. A steady stream of cars passed beside the lot. He craned his neck leftward, waiting for the Cass Street light to turn red. The traffic lights, he knew, were set to let cars flow in long pulses suc-ceeded by short periods of relief. Nearly empty for a few seconds, the street opened to Daley and the dead car.

"Shit, man," laughed the mechanic, as he heard Daley's woeful story. "Why didn't you just come down here, buy a battery, carry it back and install it back in that parking lot of yours? You didn't need to push the damn car all the way down here. That's heart attack alley, pal. Hey, Joe! Come here!"

A second grease-stained gas station attendant walked over, simulta-neously scratching a match to light a cigarette.

"You know what this guy did? Hah! His battery went dead, so he pushed his car all the way down Fort Street through rush hour to get it charged."

"No shit!" said Joe. "Now I've heard everything." He turned to Daley Strumm. "Where you from?"

"What?"

"Where you from?"

"Well," said Daley, "I was born in Mt. Pleasant. My parents were teaching at Central. We moved to Kalamazoo when I was in kindergar-ten and lived there five years. My Mom and Dad were teaching in a little

Baptist college there. Then my folks got jobs at Michigan State in East Lansing. When I was in high school, we moved out to Williamston. So I've lived all around Michigan."

"I didn't want your fuckin' life story. What I meant was, where you come from, they got cars?"

Suddenly it dawned on Daley that the guy was baiting him. He was never comfortable in this kind of situation. Daley was sure he lacked the common touch. Again fleetingly, he wondered if this was part of the test — did Vipes put these jerks up to taunting him? How does a person with the common touch respond to such impudence?

"Yes," Strumm said. "Where I grew up we had cars, but they didn't use batteries."

"No shit!"

"That's right, no shit, either. My dad's an inventor. He solved the shit problem by inventing a new kind of food. They serve it at all the dorms at Michigan State now. It leaves absolutely no residue. One hundred percent efficient. No waste, no shit. Want some?"

"Yeah!"

"I'll trade you a case of it for a battery."

"Aw, fuck, you're puttin' us on! Jesus Christ, I can't believe I swallowed that one."

"I'm a writer," said Daley. "Sometimes I make things up." Strumm wondered if he'd exhibited the common touch with his cock-and-bull tale.

Meanwhile, unsure whether to be angry or to laugh, Joe walked back to the shop, shaking his head.

His partner, Frank, said he thought the car's battery was shot and offered to install a new battery, but he was pretty busy and if Daley wanted a rush on it, it was going to cost a heap of money.

"How much?" Daley said.

Frank blinked, sizing up Daley Strumm. "Afraid you pissed off old Joe there."

"How much is the battery?"

"Installed?"

"Whatever it takes."

"I'll give you three bronze buckos on your old one."

"And then? How much?"

"Could run a hundred."

"I work for the Detroit Filibuster," said Strumm. "Cost is no object to us."

"Filibuster? Nasty rag. Might run quite a bit over a hundred," Frank said.

"With the old battery?"

"Yep."

"Seems steep."

"Cost is no object, remember."

Strumm could feel that the mechanic thought he was moving in for the kill. Revenge through overcharging. Oddly, Daley somehow felt exhilarated. As if he were on Frank's team. Yes, he was getting some satisfaction out of sticking it to the Filibuster, too.

"I'm not worried about the price. Just hurry it up, okay?"

"Roger-dodger," Frank said. "In that case, I'll drop everything."

Strumm waited, sitting on a wooden chair next to the cash register. He leafed through an old copy of Penthouse and smelled the stench of ancient, stubbed-out but hard-to-forget cigarettes.

"Hey, Filibuster!" Frank yelled. "You want me to do something about this cracked window?"

Strumm stood, and walked into the garage. Sure enough, one of the rear side windows on the wagon was cracked. Had it been cracked before? Strumm didn't think so, but couldn't be sure. He doubted Frank would deliberately break the window. What reason would he have to commit a deliberate act of malice?

"I'll put some see-through tape on that bugger, keep the crack from spreading," Frank said. "Just charge you time, no parts."

"Okay," said Strumm, as he watched the repairman lower the wagon's back seat so he could install tape from inside the car. "Hey, Frank! Keep that battery rebate, all right? Think of it as a sort of tip. From the Filibuster."

Fifteen minutes later, Strumm was tooling down Interstate XCIV, headed west toward Calvary and beginning to organize his approach to the story. It was dawning on him that this was a real, live — well, for the moment, anyway — execution. He wasn't sure he had the stomach for it. Could he retain his professionalism when faced with the harshness of a governmental murder? Daley Strumm, you see, was fundamentally opposed to capital punishment in any form.

There was a loud pop, and the rear passenger compartment was filled with thousands of shards of imploding glass. The car fishtailed, slowed. Daley pulled onto the shoulder.

Guess the tape didn't work, Daley thought. Maybe I should have paid for a new window.

At a service station in Ypsilanti, an old man, not given either to joking or poking fun, installed a temporary repair — a clear piece of plastic secured with heavy doses of the universal fix-it material known as duct tape.

Not much else happened on the way, except that around Watervliet a ten-point buck made his decision to bound across the interstate a microsecond too late and smashed through the wagon's windshield. Daley was doing sixty-five, so the force of the car moving ahead drove the deer backward, into the car. The buck knocked off the rearview mirror, nudged Daley's right shoulder, rolled over the back of the driver's seat and flopped onto the floor of the wagon. The buck lay collapsed in the rear of the wagon, knocked out cold.

Strumm could not have avoided the accident. He'd caught sight of the buck just as it was bounding across the concrete highway. There was no time even to touch the brakes. With the now smashed windshield sending glass all over his lap and across the front seat, Daley had lost track of the deer. He could see (quite clearly, in fact, because there was no glass between him and the outdoors) that the hood of the wagon was undamaged. He stopped, jumped out, brushed the glass off his clothes, folded his coat and laid it on the seat to cushion his posterior from small shards of glass, got back in and drove on. The wind hitting his face felt fresh and invigorating; he decided that since the Gethsemane Bureau of the Filibuster was only half an hour away, he'd arrange for a new windshield when he arrived. He wouldn't worry about it now.

He wondered what had become of the deer.

Pretty resilient animals, he thought. No doubt, the deer had loped into the woods with a fur-raising new yarn to tell his spouse.

It never occurred to Daley to inspect the cargo area of the wagon.

What a trip! What more could possibly happen?

This time, Daley thought, I won't let myself get depressed. I couldn't help hitting the deer. The battery wasn't my fault, either, or the back window.

There's still time to pull something good out of this assignment. I'll do the best I can, that's all I can do.

Now, on to Calvary.

chapter XVIII

JUST A CRUCIFIXION

In the Filibuster newsroom, the ringing of the telephone — Daley Strumm's call for aid — went unanswered, but not unheard. Several people were aware the telephone was ringing. . . and ringing. . . and ringing. There is a certain point when a telephone rings, apparently without cease, when those who have already decided not to answer the phone become angry at its continued ringing.

It takes a certain nerve, a certain ballsy disregard for the aural comfort of others to let a phone keep ringing like that, thought Chutney Vipes.

Don Strodum's thoughts ran more along the line of wondering what kind of person could afford the luxury of spending five minutes idly waiting for a telephone not to be answered.

For both editors had much bigger fish to fry than picking up and speaking into a mere telephone.

Vipes and Strodum were frantically trying to locate David Caninski — had been trying for the past hour to find the publisher.

"We're shit out of luck," pronounced Strodum. "Where the hell could he be?"

Their combined failure to find the publisher seemed less disastrous to Vipes, who viewed Caninski's disappearance as a reprieve. He was late in writing his forced confession explaining why he'd done such a dumb thing as assign Caesar O'Toole to cover the crucifixion. As long as Caninski was out of the building, the publisher was in no position to read a memo that had not yet been written.

Chutney had just spent a few delightful minutes with Minky Maloney, who had, among other things, inspired him with a great way to featurize the crucifixion.

But it would take Caninski to pull it off.

"That's entertainment," Minky had said. She had stroked the fine brown hairs on his arm as she outlined her scheme: Get Caninski to lean on his good buddy Pontius Pilate, who in turn would order the state police to "give Jesus a break."

The idea was as simple as it was brilliant, and would work perfectly into the lifestyle section of the paper, known as "The Way We Are," or TWWA for short.

"How long has he been nailed up there?" asked Minky. She fluttered her eyelids over those pale blue eyes of hers in a way that convinced Chutney the idea was the best approach yet to this story.

"Everybody needs a break now and then — sometimes even a regular break," said Minky.

"So, why not give this guy a break from dying on the cross? If the troopers would just un-nail — is that right? How do you say remove the nails?"

"Pull them," Vipes said.

"Yes, pull the nails for a short time and let him down for a little walk. Of course, our reporter would be there for an exclusive interview. I think we could afford to let Daley wine and dine him a bit, don't you? Take him to some little café not far from the cross and let him have his last supper."

"You know," mused Chutney, turning on his side and staring into Minky's pink face. "That idea has some merit. We could even go further — I'm thinking on the grand scale now. This guy Jesus has a crew of friends, a dozen or so miscreants who are sticking by him. Why not invite them, too? Then we photograph the tableau, write a big story, and we've got an exclusive. 'The Last Lunch.' Yes, Minky, I like it. I like it very much."

Minky rose from the couch and began putting her brassiere on. "Just don't forget whose idea it was, Chut. I want it for my section."

Back in the newsroom, Strodum had tried the idea on with his usual irrepressible humor.

"A break from cross duty, huh? Hope the guy doesn't mind—ha-ha! Hope he's not cross!"

"The whole idea hangs on Pilate's good will." Vipes laughed. "Hope he doesn't double-cross us!"

"No, it hangs on our finding the goddam publisher of this newspaper," said Strodum. "Where the hell could he be?"

At the moment, David Caninski was driving his black Cadillac limo through rush hour traffic on Woodward and talking heatedly on his cellular car phone.

At the other end of the telephone line, Detroit Police Chief Wilbur Manning listened to the Filibuster publisher's tirade.

"Duh, you just turn him loose to me, Wilbur — I'll duh take care of punishing the dirty little duh s.o.b. Words fail me here, Wilbur, duh when faced with the duh enormity of his duh peccadillo, but I assure you that duh it will be the last time a duh Filibuster columnist uses such duh poor judgment that he duh gets caught with his duh pants down."

Nobody knows how hard the life of a major metropolitan newspaper publisher can be except those rare birds, the publishers themselves. It is a hard lot that even their million-bucko salaries and abundant stock purchase plans can do little to ameliorate.

Take, for example, this particular Friday. First, David Caninski had dined on veal scaloppine with caviar, chef salad and sixty-year-old wine that did little to ease him through the ethical quandary set before him by his old college roommate, Pontius Pilate. Sure, Dave had done a reprehensible thing by agreeing to squelch the Filibuster's coverage of a legitimate news story, but do you think that made the publisher feel good about himself? Next, he had written about it in his Sunday confessional column, except that in the end, honestly, he found he could not write about it in a way that would edify readers and glorify the Filibuster, so he was forced to evade all the important issues, as usual.

It was just a typical publisher's day. There had been the minor incident in the newsroom, when he overheard the faithful Caesar O'Toole telling his wife about the unspeakable assignment he'd pulled. It had been easy enough, as publisher, to fix that. But to do it, he'd had to sting his city editor. That was never a wise thing to do. City editors were good people to keep happy. Until the time came, as it inevitably would come, of course, to fire him or title him into oblivion. The Filibuster had a whole mausoleum full of former news editors, copy desk chiefs and city editors who now sulked around under the weight of titles such as "Assistant to the Deputy Executive Editor for Change" or "Deputy to the Assistant Managing Editor for Scope."

So he'd have to rap Vipes' knuckles, an act made all the more unpleasant because of what he had found out about Vipes and Minky Maloney — a knowledge he would soon be forced to act upon. Oh, yes, there would be some pleasure, for the publisher already had a title in mind for Chutney when the time came to axe him — "Assistant Deputy Editor for Integrity." The thought made Caninski smile. The perfect title for Vipes — all gas, no substance.

But his pleasure was fleeting. It had already been a hard day, even before Mutt Prescott's call for a ride to work.

It had sounded innocent enough. Mutt Prescott, the star sports columnist, needed a ride to work. Now, most meek and humble employees of the Filibuster, upon finding their car was somehow unavailable to get them to their job, would probably have called for a cab. Or taken a bus. But perhaps Mutt was used to getting his favors directly from the publisher in the form of Sunday columnary paeans of praise and ten-thousand-bucko bonuses when rumors fanned by Mutt got round that the News and Free Press had made him a job offer. At any rate, Mutt did not call a cab.

Well, perhaps in all fairness he did not behave as a common man because he knew that in this instance he really needed all the help he could get from the publisher. For it had come to pass in those days that a certain king named Herod Cole had decreed that anyone caught trading in flesh — i.e., using a prostitute — would be jailed and his car, as the scene of the unlawful activity, impounded and auctioned off. Proceeds of such sales were used to fund the latest restoration of Herod's vacation spa on Mackinac Island.

So it was that David Caninski was treated to a series of blunt shocks that afternoon. First, there was the call from Mutt asking for a ride because he couldn't find his car. Then came the search for the Third Precinct Police Station, where David Caninski was supposed to pick Mutt up. Caninski assumed Mutt had gone there to report his car stolen. Following his arrival at the police station, he was directed to go downtown to the District Court magistrate's chambers.

It seemed strange that a case of car theft would be solved and the culprits arraigned within hours of the crime report, but what did David Caninski know? Not much about the crime beat, which he'd never covered as a young editor-in-waiting. In the crumbling courtroom painted in sickly gray and pink he had watched accused murderers, rapists, arsonists and child abusers stand, one by one, hands clasped behind their backs, as charges were read against them.

There, suddenly, he had watched in shock as a blue-uniformed bailiff unlocked a pair of handcuffs so Mutt Prescott could stand behind a short lectern and hear what the Detroit Police Department had to say about him.

But the proceedings did not proceed any further.

David Caninski had first swiveled his head all around, making sure there were no vermin — that is, newspaper reporters — lurking about. Then he was on his feet, thumping toward the door of the court holding tank.

"Ah am duh David Caninski, this man's employer and duh I demand to know why he is duh being treated like a duh common criminal," the publisher said.

The bailiff, a squat, muscular man with a broad jaw and receding black hair, gave Caninski a push. "Because he is a duh common criminal," the bailiff said in a surprisingly good imitation of the publisher.

"Ah demand that you duh delay this proceeding so that this man may be duh represented by an attorney," Caninski said.

Of course, the magistrate recognized Caninski from the head photo that ran with his weekly column. The proceedings were stayed, quickly and quietly.

Now, on his car phone, Caninski berated the police chief. "Don't you be a duh fool, Wilbur," said Caninski. "You keep Mutt in that tank a minute longer and I promise you that duh I will aim the full might of the newspaper I command at having you duh removed summarily or duh however long it may take from a job that a duh hardworking boy like you never dreamed of having in the duh first place."

There was a slight pause as the chief, who happened to be black, took in the racial slur in Caninski's use of the words "hardworking boy."

"Sorry, Dave, no can do."

"Yes, Wilbur, can do! Can do! Right duh now, duh immediately!"

"You'll have to take it up with my superior."

"Okay, you tell that duh cherub-faced king of yours I want to talk to him duh pronto!"

"Nobody talks to Herod pronto, Dave, least of all the papers. I don't think King Herod likes you guys. You make fun of the way he catches fish."

"He catches fish without a duh license, Wilbur, and that's no way for a king to behave."

"Well, maybe, Dave, but you shouldn't ought to have written that mean editorial about him. He's mad."

"We took a legitimate duh swipe at him for violating the conservation law of this state. What would you have us duh do? Ignore the infraction because it was duh committed by the king?"

"And what would you have Herod do now — overturn his crackdown on whores and johns by letting your star thumb-sucker off the hook? What if the News and Free Press got ahold of that story? It would not be politically smart of the king to help you out, Dave."

"Politically smart! I'll tell you duh what is politically smart. If you weren't Herod's bastard son, you wouldn't have the duh title you hold right now as duh chief law enforcement duh officer of this city."

"You are a blunt one, Dave. I think you better talk to Herod about who's his bastard son."

Caninski hung up, thinking, by God, this has all the duh earmarks of a bad day. I better duh take positive action so this duh negativity does not bleed into duh my weekend. Caninski punched in Herod's private number and began speaking to the king's press secretary.

Because it was not possible to reach David Caninski at this particular moment in his career, Don Strodum and Chutney Vipes decided to take matters into their own hands. Based on their knowledge that Caninski and Pontius Pilate were old friends, shared a cottage and were trying to get rich fast together in the gold mine business, the pair of editors decided not to wait for Caninski to give Pilate a call.

"You call Pilate," Strodum said. "You're the city editor."

chapter XIX

DOUBLE CROSS

Pontius Pilate could not believe his ears. It was just stupid enough to be a prank, but Pilate had met Chutney Vipes and knew the man's voice. It really was the city editor of the Filibuster and thus it was no trick.

Sorry to bother him at home, says Vipes. But the Filibuster is brewing up a big story. A crucifixion story with all the stops pulled out, says Vipes. Religion writer Daley Strumm assigned to cover execution.

And the man actually said he needed a favor! A favor to help him slap his crucifixion story into the paper with a little more pizzazz, panache and a few other choice words intended to impress him with the importance of his, Pilate's, role in creating this blockbuster news story.

What planet did this man live on? Did Dave Caninski really work at the Filibuster? What kind of control did he exercise over these morons he hired to put out his paper?

He, Pontius Pilate, had spent more than $C on lunch to convince his old friend that stifling the crucifixion story was of the utmost importance. That his, Pontius Pilate's, whole future relations with the King of Detroit, Herod Cole, depended upon killing news coverage of this event. What Herod wanted, Pilate perforce would deliver — execution, public relations, the whole ball of wax.

Now what was he hearing? The Filibuster was trying to milk a Pulitzer Prize out of the crucifixion of one insignificant religious screwball!

We know you're friends with David Caninski, said Vipes. Correction, WERE friends, thought Pilate.

No way could Dave not be a party to this. In spite of his pleading over lunch and even leaving the tip, Dave was conspiring to stab him in the back.

Unbelievable!

Pilate punched in Dave's number. Caninski's secretary took the call.

Mr. Caninski cannot be reached at the moment.

You bet he cannot be reached at the moment. He'd better hope he can't be reached at the moment. A lower, meaner, nastier peace of skulduggery and backstabbery Pilate had never seen, and that included some pretty foul tricks — midnight raps on the door and root cellar murders — Pilate had conceived on behalf of the federal government.

His next call was to his broker, who was in.

"Bill, I want all my shares in Fandango Gold put on the market, right now."

Next, he called his real estate agent. "List my half of the Lake St. Clair cottage. I want it on the market as soon as possible."

Next, Pilate called his wife. "Forget that beach party with the Caninskis," he snarled.

Having acted out of vengeance three times, Pilate finally moved to take preventive action. He called Col. Edward Height, commander of the Michigan State Police.

"Hi, Ed, how goes it? Yeah, she's fine, kids are fine. Herod? Well, that's why I'm calling, Ed. I'm doing a little public relations work here, preventive PR, you might say. There's a reporter from the Filibuster headed out to Calvary to write up the crucifixion of Jesus Christ. Name's Strumm, Daley Strumm. Daley is spelled D-A-L-E-Y. Strumm is spelled S-T-R-U-M-M. Daley Strumm. Can your boys make sure Daley Strumm doesn't get there? Terminal? What does that mean, 'terminal'? 'Extreme' what? 'Prejudice'? No, not quite that far. Just detain him. Make him miss the story. Hey, thanks, Ed, I owe you one."

chapter XX

ONLY THE BEST (RESTAURANTS)

Talk about your authority problems! They were rampant out in the Filibuster's Gethsemane Bureau due to a want of editorial supervision. Ever since he was appointed city editor five years ago, Chutney Vipes had been meaning to pull a surprise visit to the Gethsemane Bureau in western Michigan. But word was that the restaurants out that way weren't so great, and for some reason only one female reporter (and she a cantankerous sort not given to hobnobbing with the brass or simple courteous flirting) was posted in that boondocks office. But visiting a bureau full of cynical, burned-out, middle-aged male reporters whose bleak futures were preordained by a hybrid system of star promotion and ethnic Darwinism was not Vipes' idea of a fun outing. And the one female reporter was an exiled ingrate whose repeated attempts to introduce unconventional reporting were a thorn in Vipes' side. It was sad, really. A once fast-track career: A black female destined — if she played her cards right — to high office in the chain that owned the Filibuster had squandered that advantage through a stubborn penchant for originality. At the Filibuster, no idea was a good one that had not been previously tested and found safe at ten or twenty other media outlets.

Thus, Vipes had never managed to bring off a visit.

It was just as well. The bureau was hell on editors.

To give an idea of the greeting an editor would face, one only need glance at the custom-printed poster a Gethsemane reporter had thumbtacked over his desk.

**NO STORY IS SO WELL WRITTEN
THAT A GOOD EDITOR CAN'T FUCK IT UP.**

Another one-of-a-kind poster said,

**SOME STORIES ARE SO FUCKED UP
ONLY AN EDITOR WOULD FAIL TO NOTICE**

Then, there was this incredibly jaded travesty drawn onto a huge
piece of pasteboard:

Editor's Troubleshooting Flowchart

This was the journalistic environment Daley Strumm entered following his nightmare trip from Detroit. Vipes' instructions were that he should use the Gethsemane Bureau as a base for his reporting because the office was only thirty minutes by freeway from Calvary, where the crucifixion was to take place.

It was good luck, really, that the Filibuster had a news bureau so close to the execution. Daley wondered briefly why one of the three Gethsemane reporters had not been given the assignment. After all, they were nearby — why, they could have been at the scene hours ago, even had a story written by now and be on their way home to families and dinner!

Of course, the bureau reporters didn't stop to wonder two seconds about the apparent managerial slight. Paranoiacs that they were, these reporters were sure that editors and reporters downtown — at the Big Paper — were conspiring to give all the choice Gethsemane assignments to star reporters stationed in the newsroom. People like Blaine Monihan, Peg Morris, Babe Everest.

At any rate, Daley Strumm stopped in his tracks just as he stepped over the threshold of the office doorway.

Incredible! It was Caninski's voice — Caninski was here!

"Duh Parker, I'd like you to arrange duh free ringside seats for an upcoming crucifixion and duh hang the expense duh no pun intended!"

"But Dave," another voice said, "accepting free tickets would violate the ethical guidelines of the Filibuster. You wrote those guidelines yourself."

"You're duh mistaken, Parker, though I don't duh hold that against you. I wrote those ethical duh guidelines for reporters to duh comport themselves by and duh they do not apply to someone on my duh exalted level at the Filibuster."

"But Mr. Caninski, don't you believe in setting an example for your, uh, employees?"

"'Lackeys' is duh the word you were most likely duh groping for, Parker, and no I duh do not feel the least bit hypocritical in duh laying down rules of duh comportment for my employees while adhering to duh a different set of standards myself. That is my duh prerogative, Parker, because I earn in excess of a million smackers a year. And now duh before you ask me any more dumb-ass questions, let me duh describe to you the options that I duh have in regard to your future at this newspaper."

"But Dave, if you're talking about punishing me, how is that possible? You've already banished me to the Gethsemane Bureau, where I've languished for seven years. What more can you do to me?"

"Duh, Parker, allow me to describe for you the delights of covering night cops."

Daley Strumm walked farther into the office, which was L-shaped and thus capable of hiding the owners of the two voices until the visitor had made the turn.

What he saw was not David Caninski, the publisher, but a tall, gangly man with yellow hair and a face so average, so nondescript as to be almost completely forgettable. This tall man pretending to be David Caninski was talking to a thin man with a beard and glasses. The mimic was a reporter named Robert Saunter. The straight man was Parker Haynes. Daley Strumm had walked into the pair's daily comedy hour, which sometimes began at nine and ended at six.

At sight of Strumm, Saunter broke off his imitation.

In an intentionally unctuous tone, Saunter said, "May I help you?"

"Yes, I'm Daley Strumm. I'm supposed to be covering the crucifixion of a fellow named Jesus Christ, aka Jesus of Nazareth."

"Oh, yes, Mr. Strumm," Saunter said in an oozing voice that led Daley to suspect mockery at every level.

"We've been expecting you," Saunter said. "My friend Chutney Vipes, our city editor, told us all about you and the crucifixion. Yes, indeed. Funny thing. We've been filing stories about the Messiah for years, but they never get in the paper. Maybe we don't know how to write them. I suppose a reporter from downtown may be able to show us how it should be done. We're just hoping to learn so much from you, Mr. Strumm."

Strumm, whose senses were somewhat deadened, nonetheless thought he detected sarcasm. "Hey, I didn't ask for the assignment, and I'd just as soon not be doing it," said Strumm.

"I'm so sorry you've been forced to slum out here," said Saunter. "Reporters in this bureau are not accustomed to picking and choosing their stories. Ours is not to question why, ours but to write and spike. Please don't take what I'm saying personally, Mr. Strumm. All the same, it sure will be interesting after all these tries if a star writer from the big paper downtown can get it onto the front page. Maybe this is my big chance to learn from a pro."

"Look," said Strumm. "I just drove four and a half hours through unbelievable hell. They sent me to meet a helicopter. The helicopter flew off without me. They gave me a Filibuster car and the battery was dead. On the highway a rear window blew out — "

"You mean the back tire, don't you?" said Saunter.

"I mean the window blew out!" said Strumm.

"You mean to tell me you had a blowout on your window? Maybe you filled it too full of air!"

"Then I hit a deer, or a deer hit me — "

"Okay, okay, it's a miserable assignment even without the bad luck stories. We'll lay off. . . won't we Park?"

"We'll even help, Daley," said Parker Haynes. "First by telling you to call Vipes ASAP. Something about getting the guy off the cross so you can take him to lunch. And how there isn't a good lunch place in all of Gethsemane. Of course, how would Vipes know? Anyway, we'll even tell you where you can go for lunch."

Daley punched in the city desk number and waited. This time, his call was answered promptly by a copy aide.

"Chutney Vipes is here, but he's left word we're not to bother him. He's writing a memo to Caninski," the aide said.

"Is Don Strodum there?"

"No — well, yes, he's in the building, but he's not at his desk."

"Can you transfer me to him?"

"No, I can't — he's leading a tour of the building for some journalism students. No idea quite where he is."

Daley hung up. "Amazing," he said. "Vipes is incommunicado writing a memo and the deputy city editor is leading a guided tour of the Filibuster building."

"First useful thing either of those guys did," said Parker Haynes.

Daley interrupted Robert Saunter just as the big reporter with the malleable face was making certain body moves leading into his famed imitation of Chutney Vipes. "Where's this restaurant where you think I should take the guy?"

"Well," said Saunter, "There's a very elegant little Argentinean place at the foot of Calvary Hill. It's a bit pricey, but if the Filibuster is paying, cost is not a concern of yours. There's also a bar, Iscariot's, but it's just a tad on the proletarian side, if you know what I mean. Mainly steelworkers from the Gethsemane mill. But then Jesus used to work in that mill, and the owner of that bar is one of his disciples, so I imagine he'd feel at home there."

"Well, maybe I'd better try one more time to get through to Vipes," Daley said. He remembered Vipes had lent him a company cell phone. He pulled the phone from his pants pocket. As he did so, he noticed Parker Haynes turn in his chair and stare at him. Haynes was drumming his fingertips on his desk as if he couldn't wait for something to happen.

Daley hit the ON button. Haynes stared as Daley punched in the city desk number. He got a busy signal.

Haynes leapt to his feet. "You got a busy, didn't you? Hah! How many times do I have to tell people? Nobody listens!"

"Tell people what?" asked Daley.

"He gets excited when people use cell phones around here," explained Saunter. "Parker's been pitching the story for years. Cell phones don't work in Gethsemane."

"They damned well don't work, and for good reason," said Haynes. "People are fucking with them, that's why. Either they blow up the towers, or they jam them. You want to hear what jamming sounds like?"

"Daley doesn't have time for that." Saunter turned to Daley. "It's true, though. Parker has an amazing story, well documented, about how terrorists with a sinister agenda have shut down cell communications in western Michigan."

"What's their sinister agenda?" asked Daley.

"Very simple," said Haynes. "They want people to drive safely. If cell phones don't work, people will quit using them. That means they quit talking into them while they drive. The number of traffic fatalities has fallen, but statistics don't matter. Nobody else will run the story. That means the Filibuster won't run it, either. Somebody's got to be first, and it won't be our paper."

"That means nobody will run it," said Saunter.

"It might have something to do with those big ads we sell to the phone companies," mused Daley.

"How cynical of you," said Saunter. "You're not pulling together in the clutch."

"I don't care why the paper won't run it, I just want to write it," said Haynes.

"Just like I want to write about Herod's shakedown business," chimed in another voice. This was Sarah Bukari. "They want to prove they're not racists by shit-canning the work of a black woman as well as a white man. They're equal-opportunity bastards."

"Now come on, Sarah," said Saunter. "Don't start on that again. Anybody who's white and male around here has a target on his back. As soon as one of us goes, they get to hire a young black woman and reap their Editing By Goals bonus. Guys like Parker and me are money down the drain in their book."

"If you play the game, Rob, if you play the game, white or black, you can get ahead," said Sarah. "But the ones who pocket the bonuses for moving minorities around are old white guys."

Now, Daley noticed another person in the bureau. This was a small, dark-haired woman who sat quietly gazing at color photos on a computer screen. She was Natalie Poole, the bureau photographer. Odd that none of the bureau reporters, so sensitive to having been supplanted by Daley as crucifixion reporters, ever considered that Natalie Poole might feel the same way about having the prima donna Carla Strumpff galumphing around her beat. Natalie took no part in the bitch session, but for a moment she turned and looked thoughtfully at the four reporters verbally duking it out. Her large black eyes took in the scene and then focused on her images. Perhaps the placard over her desk explained Natalie's philosophy on the difference between reporters and photographers at the Filibuster:

Reporter's Troubleshooting Flowchart

Daley could see he'd stumbled into the quotidian bitching session. These three bureau reporters were the butts of somebody's bad joke. Social engineering run amok. Stymied, unable to figure a way out of it, they spun their wheels in useless bickering. He tuned out, picked up a landline phone, thought for a moment, and put it down. *On second thought, why waste my time?*

And a waste of time it would have been, too, at that moment. For Chutney Vipes had finally come to grips with the single solid piece of work he had before him that Friday afternoon — Dave Caninski's godawful demand for an explanatory, humiliating memo. Vipes let himself into a small office at the west end of the newsroom. It was an office used mainly by the award-winning team of investigative reporters when they wanted to sneak a cigarette in violation of the company smoking ban. The place smelled like dead cigars, but Vipes didn't mind. It was quiet, and he'd left strict orders that he wasn't to be disturbed.

Vipes sat down at a computer screen. For several minutes, he simply stared at the glass rectangle. Finally, he struck two keys. LO for Logon.

Space. CHUT. Execute. Now for the secret password, which nobody was supposed to guess because it was taken from the depths of each user's innermost being. Vipes tapped the keys. CLIMB.

Instantly, the header was up for his queue. It flashed MSG PENDING.

Vipes hit the keys, RD MSG

His jaw sagged. His first thought was that it was a trick, maybe Strodum's doing. He scrolled to the bottom, found the CANIN signer.

Damn! This was real. *Cancel all crucifixion coverage!*

Where was Bontemps? Where was Strodum?

By Jupiter, Strumm might be at Calvary by now! Strumpff was most certainly there, with a chopper standing by to rush her back to the paper. How long had this order been hanging? The time was registered on the header: One-forty-five post meridian. Right after lunch. Caninski had ordered this stop hours ago. Why hadn't he, the city editor, been told?

Suddenly, Vipes realized that he had been told — this message told him. He had simply not bothered to log onto the computer since before his amorous lunch date with Minky. After lunch, he'd been far too busy planning crucifixion coverage. True, there'd been interludes with Minky in her private office, at personnel with the Wolfman file, but that was all dogwork necessary to carrying out the function of his city editor's job. He could hardly be blamed for doing his duty. Chutney grabbed the phone, punched in the area code and the Gethsemane Bureau number. He was panicked. God, if Caninski finds out we've got people out there eating up expense money on a story he's shit-canned, my ass is grass!

"Filibuster, Bob Saunter," a voice purred.

"Bob, did Strumm make it to Gethsemane?"

"Yes, Chutney, he certainly did. Most certainly did."

These bureau reporters were a constant frustration. So laid-back, with their charming telephone voices, unhassled. It must be nice to be far from the action, the pressure, the conniving, the striving for bigger and better titles and salaries. But they did get on an editor's nerves with their relaxed, no-care-in-the-world attitudes.

"Give me Strumm right now!"

"Well, gee, Chutney, he's not here."

"I thought you said he was."

"I said he certainly made it here, Chutney. That's what you asked me, if I recall properly."

"Oh, Jesus, Saunter! I don't care how he made it."

"That's too bad, Chutney. Because he did have a terrible time making it here. Very strange story. Did you ever hear of a blowout on a window? Daley Strumm had one. No wonder you put the man on the religion beat — he works miracles."

"Will you quit fooling around? Where is he?"

"Well, Chutney, the last I saw of Daley Strumm, he was driving away from our office in a car that lacked a windshield. And there was a deer sitting in the back seat. I think he might have gotten here faster if he hadn't picked up a hitchhiker."

"What are you talking about? Will you try to make sense?"

"I'll try, Chutney."

"Okay, where did he go?"

"I don't know. For sure."

"Well, take a guess."

"Well, I think his assignment was to cover a crucifixion at Calvary Hill. So my guess would be that he went there to carry out his assignment."

"I know that! I'm the one who gave him the assignment!"

"Well, gosh, Chutney, if that's the case, why are you asking me where he is?"

"Because there's no way in hell I'll ever find him at Calvary. He doesn't have a radio. He doesn't have a pager. He's all alone."

"He does have that cell phone you gave him."

There was a moment of silence as Vipes tried to remember the number of that phone.

"And he does have the deer, Chutney."

"I don't care about the deer! What deer? Where'd he get a deer? Why'd he get a deer?"

"I don't know, Chutney. I wondered about those things myself. I didn't think to ask him."

"Why not? What kind of a reporter are you? For Pluto's sake, no wonder Dave sent you out to Gethsemane. You're incompetent! If Strumm's got a deer — oh, hell! I don't care about deer! Look, Saunter, do me a big favor. When he comes back, or if Carla Strumpff comes back, you tell them — make certain you make this very clear — there's no coverage of the crucifixion. None whatsoever. Not a single line. Not one picture. Got that? Read it back to me: What did I say?"

"Don't you remember?"

"Dammit, Saunter, I want to make sure you understand me!"

"Well, you said, 'Look Saunter, when he comes back or if Carla Strumpff comes back — '"

"Okay, okay, I don't have time to hear a transcript." A thought struck Vipes. Well, not so much a thought as a hunger pang. Time to hunt Minky up and head for a restaurant. The Chop House, maybe.

"Hey, Saunter, did Strumm eat before he got to Gethsemane?"

"I don't know. I doubt it. The deer looked pretty much in one piece."

"You dumbie — the deer has nothing to do with anything. It's not part of this story! And this story isn't part of the story. It's been spiked, by Caninski himself. Now listen: Strumm was supposed to take Christ to dinner. You guys out there start calling restaurants. Think of the best restaurants — if there are any — and have him paged."

"There must be some best restaurants out here, Chut."

"Not necessarily. Melanie Munch doesn't think so."

"But comparatively speaking, Chut, even if they're all pretty lousy, some are bound to be lousier than others, which makes the others better. And of the ones that are better, some would be lousier so the ones that aren't lousier would be the best. See what I mean?"

"No. Just think: Where would you take this guy if it was up to you?"

"You mean if you'd assigned a bureau reporter like me who knows all the cops and judges and mayors around Calvary and has been writing stories about these political and religious crucifixions for years although they never make the paper? Well, if it were me, I'd take him to a nice little Argentinean place near Calvary."

"I don't care for South American — " Vipes, whose mouth was watering at the talk about restaurants, suddenly remembered they were speaking of Daley Strumm and not his own plans for dinner.

"Check that Argentinean place first, then."

"Also, there's a bar nearby called Iscariot's. He might have gone there."

"No, he wouldn't go to a bar, Saunter. Jesus is a religious martyr! Martyrs don't frequent bars. Besides, Strumm is a religion writer — he wouldn't be caught in a tavern. Besides, he's on an expense account. Nobody in his right mind on an expense account goes to a cheap bar when they can write off a big meal to the Filibuster. You just check the ritzy restaurants."

"Roger, Chutney. Look for Strumm in best restaurants, not bars. As you say."

chapter XXI

SITTING ON A PULITZER

Groups of men, women and children in twos and threes walked the streets of Gethsemane, all moving in the same direction. Daley Strumm assumed they were headed for Calvary. By order of Pontius Pilate and Herod "Old King" Cole, the executions were open to the public, free of charge. Cost of the performances — price of wooden crosses, spikes, police overtime, etc. — was being offset by the sale of special state lottery tickets.

The strategy was simple: Crucifixions attract spectators who spend money on lotto tickets. And lotteries attract speculators who, out of curiosity or boredom while waiting in line to buy their tickets, also watch the crucifixion. So what if some of these spectators take part in a little illicit gambling? That can't be helped — these multiple cross executions are fantastic ad hoc betting opportunities, a weird sort of horse race where the winner is the last to expire.

But the gambling is a sideshow. In the number one ring is Justice, i.e., stamping out crime. In Herod's old-fashioned view, nothing beats public executions for deterring criminals. You show your potential burglar a convicted housebreaker dying the slow death and he's liable to think twice before committing his next B & E. Of course, crucifixion was not nearly as effective a deterrent for those corrupt water commissioners, police chiefs and budget managers who surrounded Herod and were occasionally caught stealing their millions of public monies.

Such people were not really criminals in your classic sense of the word. Often they were people who had become addicted to a certain standard of living that they could not afford to maintain on their paltry public servant's salary. To execute such people would drive home the wrong point, making it clear that there was no place in government for the poor, middle-class person on the hustle.

Besides, Herod kept pretty good tabs on the books and knew, long before the IBI did, who was on the take. Such people, once compromised, were quite useful — malleable was the word, really. They could be coerced into doing most anything. If the feds happened to catch them, well, a mild but socially embarrassing stint in a federal penal colony would serve to return each of them to the world a humbler, but wiser, thief. And it would make them more dependent and thus more pliable civil servants next time around. For criminality was no deterrent to becoming a government employee. Thus, crucifixion was a punishment reserved for the classes of people who would benefit most from the lesson: DON'T GET CAUGHT!

A chill wind hit the red Filibuster station wagon and whipped through the hole the deer had made. The wind no longer invigorated Daley Strumm. His shivers were turning to shudders. He was fairly close to Calvary now — the clots of people moving toward the execution hill were getting bigger. He could hear their voices, loud, raucous. Some of them were carrying bottles of wine, beer, whiskey with no effort at concealing it.

Strumm could stand the cold no more. He had to get out of the car, warm up.

A purple-and-white sign flashed the word "Iscariot's." It might make a good place to bring Jesus if it wasn't too loud. Strumm hated loud places, whether they were bars, hotel parties or roller skating rinks.

He stopped the wagon, parked it along the curb in front of the bar. He remembered the windshield. No point locking the car, but he did just the same. Now for a burger and a Coke, get warm, then head on to Calvary.

Iscariot's was a long, narrow bar in the old tradition. Judas Iscariot, the owner, had refused to go the way of many modern tavern keepers, so there was no line of nude dancers to titillate the patrons. There was a pool table at the back of the dimly lit room and at the side a shuffleboard game. Modern bars have eliminated these niceties on the theory that games don't sell drinks as fast as the additional tables and chairs that could replace them. Judas Iscariot had held out against the tide of development. He just liked his bar the way it was, even if it wasn't a big moneymaker. He liked a game of pool, he liked shuffleboard, and he liked the kind of hardworking factory worker who came here to play and drink and talk about women. The extra money was no big deal.

But if the extra money was no big deal, why was he sitting at one of his black Formica-topped tables with two clean-cut young men in cheap business suits who were handing him a big manila envelope made fat with certificates of stocks, bonds, mutual funds and other negotiable instruments? All were in his name and totaled thirty thousand silver buckos.

Strumm came in just as the clean-cut men, who happened to be Michigan State Police detectives, were scooting their chairs back, shaking Iscariot's hand and congratulating him on having done his duty as a law-abiding citizen.

Strumm thus saw a white-haired man with a flushed face sitting at a table that looked like a stockbroker's desk. Iscariot's longish white hair was plastered greasily to his head. On the table in the midst of the papers was a big glass containing a little ice and a lot of martini. Judas Iscariot was wearing a red-and-green-tartan flannel shirt open at the throat. Curly white hairs from his chest poked their way out the sagging V of his shirt neck. His eyes were blue, but watery, vacant.

He was alone in the bar, except for Strumm.

"Whatcha want?" Iscariot asked.

"Is it possible that I might get a hamburger and a Coke?" Strumm asked.

"Sure. I can make it." The words sounded hollow, as if the mind that manipulated them was far, far away. "Just had a strange, strange experience. Strange. Exper — experience."

"Meeting with your brokers, I see," said Strumm.

"Brokers! Hah! Oh, those guys are brokers, all right. Not stocks, though. Not stocks."

Iscariot stared at Strumm until Daley realized he wasn't seeing him.

"Not stocks. No way. Their commodity is — "

Judas Iscariot broke off, shook his head.

"Where you from, son?"

"Detroit — I work for a newspaper."

"Which one? News and Free Press?"

"No, the Filibuster."

"Rag. Lemme tell you, that paper is a bunch of swine. Sorry to say it. Never could stand that Dave Camonkey. Pious hypocrite."

"True enough."

"Well, suppose you got to work somewhere. Sorry for you it's there. Have a martini?"

"No, thanks."

"On the house."

"No, thanks. I'm working."

"So am I. Doesn't stop me. What you doin' out here?"

"Reporting a crucifixion."

There was a long silence as Judas Iscariot seemed to be turning the information over and over. Finally, that phenomenon occurred which always amazed Daley Strumm. He called it the free will confession. How many times had he been sent out to interview some mother whose only son had been blotted out in a tragic car accident just hours before and found the mother not angry at the intrusion, but eager to unload her sorrows to a perfect stranger?

"I got something to say about that crucifixion," said Iscariot. "You see, it was gonna happen anyway, like the plumber."

"Plumber?"

"Yeah, somebody's got to do it, you know. And it had to be me. I knew it was my job. I just wish I could give all this stuff back. Thirty thou! That's big money to a guy like me. I work every day, still owe payments on the mortgage, behind on my car. Thirty thou! Maybe I could buy a place up north. Sell this bar, retire. Fish. Water ski. Ice-fish in the winter. Forget about him. About crucifixions."

"Could you start at the beginning? I'm not sure I follow all this."

"I sold him out! That's the beginning and that's the end of it. Of me. I see where this leads now. Oh, how I believed in him. I followed him. I got my son to watch the bar so I could travel with him on tour. I still do believe! But I sold him out. Yes, I see where this leads. I know where I'm going."

"Where?"

"Look, they came to me, those nice-looking cops. I had what they wanted. Made them a map. Garden of Gethsemane. No problem. Show you how to get there, that's easy. Easiest money you'll ever make. Hah! Easy! What a load!"

"Who is 'him'?"

"Jesus Christ! That's Who is him! Who else would be worth thirty thousand silver buckos to the state cops to bribe me to tell them where he is?"

"Oh, now I see." And, indeed, Daley did see — saw that somehow, his luck had turned, and he had blundered into a major part of the crucifixion story. Or maybe a ten-inch sidebar, file name I-BETRAY-XXIII.

But then he had another thought: This guy is in bad, bad shape. Intoxicated to a high level and depressed, terribly depressed. Daley forgot about taking notes.

"Can you get your son to come in here now and look after this place?"

"Why would I do that?"

"Well, so you could go home, take a nap. Maybe even find a minister or a priest or somebody to talk to."

"I'm talking to you right now."

"I know, but soon I'll be gone. Besides, I'm a reporter — I'm no use to you. You're carrying a heavy load of guilt and maybe you need somebody, a professional, to help you cope with it."

"Professional! I'm the professional! I got paid to be a stool pigeon. I sold out my Lord and Redeemer!"

"Well, yes and no. You did what you had to do."

"Did I?"

"Like you said, somebody had to do it. What if you hadn't directed the cops to the garden?"

"He and the other eleven disciples would still be waiting there. His credibility would be shot, because what he predicted wouldn't have happened."

"You see? You were part of a plan."

"Yeah, I know, I just feel bad about the money. It don't look right. There's the appearance of impro — impropriety."

"So, give the money to a worthy cause. A temple or the Salvation Legion. Have the last laugh on the state cops. Give their money to the Roman Civil Liberties Union."

"Hey, yeah, maybe so. Jesus, what a relief! If I don't use it for myself, it's like I never got it. My motives could be seen as pure again."

"Strumm!" It was the voice of Caesar O'Toole, whose head was peering into the dim bar. "I saw that blazing red Filibuster wagon outside," O'Toole said. "What are you doing here?" he added suspiciously.

"I'm here to cover a crucifixion."

Judas Iscariot stood up. "I'll fix that hamburger, buddy, and thanks for listening."

"You're not covering any crucifixion," said O'Toole. "That's my story. I've already interviewed the two thieves and their families. There's nothing more to do. I'm ready to write, send it back to Detroit and head home. Tidy piece of reporting for an editor, if I say so myself. So what the hell are you doing here?"

"Like I said, I'm out here to cover this crucifixion. I didn't know you were here, too."

"Hmmm, sounds like another city desk screw-up. Well, you might as well have a burger. Then you can turn around and go home."

Judas Iscariot brought a Coke for Strumm. He leaned over and whispered, "Listen buddy, that stuff about me giving that map of Gethsemane to the cops is between the two of us, okay?"

"Sure," said Strumm. "Your secret is safe with me."

"How about bringing me a Coke, too?" Caesar O'Toole said. When Judas Iscariot had returned to the bar, Caesar said, "I did that to get him out of the way, Daley. What's this about a map of Gethsemane and cops?"

"I promised him I wouldn't talk about it."

"Who is that guy, anyway?" Caesar stared at the napkin under Strumm's Coke glass and saw the gaily printed monogram: ISCARIOT'S.

"Iscariot! Not Judas Iscariot? Daley, you know what this means? You're onto a big new angle to this story! This is the guy who sold out Jesus Christ!"

"Keep your voice down, will you Caesar? He'll hear you."

"So what if he hears me? You already interviewed him, didn't you? We don't need anything more from him, so fuck him."

"I didn't interview him. We were talking, that's all."

"Same thing in the end, Daley. So you didn't take notes. You still talked to him. You know what he said. I heard about this guy. His story's on the street, man! We've got something no other media could possibly have: an exclusive interview with — with the traitor of all traitors, turncoat of turncoats, the biggest snitch of all time, the stooliest of stoolies!"

"It's off the record, Caesar. I can't use any of it."

"Like hell you can't. We're sitting on a Pulitzer, Daley. You had an incredible piece of luck landing in this of all bars to have a cheeseburger. This kind of thing happens once in a career — once in both of our careers. We're going to cash in."

"I don't see how, Caesar. The conversation was not for publication."

"Every conversation is potentially for publication, Daley. You're a journalist, you know that."

"I wasn't a journalist when I was talking to Judas. The man is seriously depressed, and he's drinking himself into a worse state. He talked to me because I was all he had. We were two human beings."

"That was then. Now you're a newspaperman with a job to do."

"No."

"Okay, Daley, I'm sorry, but I have to order you to do it."

"What do you think it would do to Judas to have all this stuff hit the papers? The man is already dying of guilt and remorse."

"I'm telling you Daley, I want that interview, and if you refuse to give it to me, I'm writing a memo for your personnel file to the effect that you disobeyed an editor's direct command. You can forget covering religion from now on. I'll get you posted to that hellhole Gethsemane Bureau, or to night cops. No more plum beats for you. Hey, you know what, Daley? I could get you fired! Now, are you going to do it?"

"I told you, no."

"Daley, your problem is you're letting your emotions cloud your journalistic objectivity. You're letting feelings get in the way of doing your job. That's a serious detriment in a reporter. It's certainly something that will be looked at with some concern by such people as Chutney Vipes and Chester Bontemps when we get back to the city desk. Think about that for a minute."

"I don't have to think about it, Caesar. I've told you how I feel."

"Okay, we're at impasse. But I see a way around it. Forget the interview you already had with him. That's off the record, quite right. Fine.

But now, based on what you got from the first interview, you go back to him and hit him with this question. You say, 'Judas, for the record, you will go down in history as the arch backstabber of all time. How does it feel?' Any response at all we'll assume confirms again the details he already gave you. That way, we get the whole conversation into the paper through the back door. You hit him with that when he comes back with your food."

Daley Strumm had stopped listening to Caesar O'Toole. He was looking around the bar, trying to see Judas Iscariot. But except for the two Filibuster men, the bar was empty.

"Oh, no! God, Caesar, I was afraid he'd hear you!"

Daley was on his feet, looking behind the bar. No Judas. At the rear of the bar he could see a door leading to basement stairs. It was dark down there. He found a switch, turned on the basement lights, hurried down the stairs. There were stacks of heavy cardboard beer cases.

Empty boxes and cardboard six-pack packages littered the floor. The cellar was small, and Daley could quickly see that Judas was not there.

He ran back up the stairs, turned down a short hallway and pushed open the door marked SHE. The women's restroom was empty.

He pushed the door marked HE. It swung six inches and bumped into something. Daley pushed again. The door moved slightly farther as the obstruction gave way, then pushed back against the door. Daley found the switch, turned on the light. He could see part of a sink, a mirror, and directly behind the top of the door, a bare lightbulb. A piece of leather was tied around a water pipe.

"Oh, no!" yelled Daley. He ran back to the bar, where he noticed Caesar O'Toole was removing the cap from a bottle of beer. "Call the police, Caesar!"

Daley grabbed a serrated bread knife and ran back to the men's room. He leaned hard against the door, forcing it to open wide enough for him to squeeze inside.

As he had feared, the leather that was tied around the pipe was a belt, and it was connected to the throat of Judas Iscariot, whose purple face with bloated tongue stared down at Strumm.

He reached up, sliced through the belt and screamed, "Caesar! Call an ambulance!"

Free of the belt, Judas' body fell stiffly, and Strumm cushioned it, laid it on the tile floor.

"Caesar!" There was no answer from O'Toole. Strumm rose, looked around frantically.

On the sink lay a piece of paper. Scrawled on it was this message:

Here hangs Judas: Traitor of Traitors, Turncoat of Turncoats and Chief Backstabber of all time.
May my Lord forgive me.

"O'Toole! Get some help!"

Daley worked his forefinger into Judas' throat, removed a small piece of martini olive. Airway clear, he thought. He knelt and pressed his mouth to Judas'. He blew a short puff. Nothing.

The door swung open. Daley knew better than to break the cadence of puff — wait — puff.

O'Toole's shadow crossed the body of Judas. The assistant city editor held a green bottle of beer and leaned against the door frame.

"Suicide, Daley. The obvious solution. Judas hangs himself and you're free to use that interview. What is that you're doing? CPR? Jesus Christ, Daley, you really are emotionally involved — that's a job for a paramedic!"

Daley turned his head, faced O'Toole. "Call a fucking ambulance, O'Toole! Now!"

The shadow that had covered Judas vanished. Daley heard O'Toole pick up the phone. Then he heard O'Toole's voice.

"Give me the city desk," O'Toole said.

chapter XXII

GLORY ANGLE

I couldn't get through to Chut, but it doesn't matter," said Caesar O'Toole. He was sitting at the bar of Iscariot's, sipping a bottle of beer. The Gethsemane police were hard-pushed to cover the near-riot and orgy surrounding what cops, as is their black-humored wont, were calling the "triple header." Nevertheless, they had come to Iscariot's, taken one look, called the county medical examiner, and departed for the big overtime show: crucifixion duty.

Daley had made a short statement to a patrolman, who said in leaving, "Stick around; the medical examiner may want some information from you two."

"Don't worry," said O'Toole. "I'm hanging out here. This'll be my office. But my reporter will have to be gone shortly."

O'Toole turned to Daley, who seemed to be staring past his shoulder. "Lucky the city desk had the foresight to send an editor out to this end. I'm on the scene and I'll run this show now, directing your reporting efforts."

Daley was silent. O'Toole had begun to notice this trait of quietude. For some reason, O'Toole sensed, Judas Iscariot's suicide had depressed Daley. Probably poor conditioning, O'Toole decided. Result of working a specialty beat like religion instead of the day-to-day cops-and-murder fare of general assignment reporting. Daley lacked the requisite hardening.

O'Toole, who was leaning his elbow against the bar top, felt something vibrate, but in his excitement ignored it. "Part of my role, as I see it now," he continued, "is to scope out the glory angle here. We have a unique opportunity to tailor our reporting to specific awards applications. Obviously, the Pulitzer is the main game in town. God, what luck that you stumbled into Iscariot's when you did; otherwise, we would have missed his suicide. It's incredible! No TV people, no local reporters, and the News and Freep nowhere to be seen. Yes, without you, Daley, we certainly would have missed a major piece of this story."

"Without me, it would never have happened," said Strumm.

"What do you mean?"

"If I hadn't come in here, he never would have talked to me. You would never have seen the Filibuster car and come in looking for me. And Iscariot would never have overheard you call him the chief backstabber of all time. He would be alive now, feeling guilty as hell, but alive to shine his bar glasses."

"He might be alive now," said O'Toole. "But maybe not. Maybe something else would have triggered his guilt complex. Somehow I think Judas was required to kill himself. Anyway, you can't blame me; he tied the belt around his own neck. So don't guilt-trip me with Judas' death. That guy was ripe for it. It's a waste of time debating what might have happened. That's history. The Pulitzer is ahead of us. Our deadline looms. Ha-ha! Our destiny is before us. Let's plan."

O'Toole fell silent. He wished he hadn't mentioned planning. Honestly, his reporting experience was so minimal that he really had no idea where or how someone would begin to cover this story. The assignment had progressed to the point where success would depend on a reporter's instincts and experience, and no amount of editorial meddling would replace having the right reporter in the field. Daley, of course, would go to Calvary, where things were happening. That's what reporters did. Beyond that, O'Toole couldn't imagine what Daley would do.

O'Toole took a long pull on his beer, then announced, "That's it! Deadline! It's part of the equation. A tiny team of Filibuster reporters arrives at Calvary with scant minutes to prepare a story. Mobs everywhere. Police with riot gear, firing tear gas. People being beaten, knocked to the ground as they try to get to scene of execution. Filibuster team, undaunted, pushes through mobs, all the time taking notes on human misery. Carla Strumpff, at considerable risk to herself, photographs police in act of brutalizing, well, whomever. It hasn't happened yet, of course, but it's bound to. Let's see, have you done anything risky on this assignment, Daley?"

"I met up with you," said Daley glumly.

"That's not what I mean," said O'Toole. "This will be my command post. I'm going to make notes on the general conditions of reporting this story, because that's what's going to sway the Pulitzer judges. I bet you've never heard of an editor actually preparing a Pulitzer nomination as the story was being produced. Well, you have now. So, if you need me, you can always find me right here," said O'Toole, as he reached into the cooler and drew out another bottle of beer.

O'Toole ignored another tremor, more forceful than the first, which clattered glasses on the bar.

"Now, as to your specific assignment, Daley, I want you to ingratiate yourself with the state police, see if you can find out how they feel about public versus private executions. Wouldn't it be safer, vis-à-vis these mobs, to conduct crucifixions secretly, or would that violate the public's right to know?"

But Daley Strumm didn't hear. He was outside, unlocking the Filibuster wagon.

Suddenly, the sidewalk heaved up. Daley was airborne for a split second, bounced off the side of the car, then slipped to the concrete. Inside Iscariot's, every bottle of liquor on Judas' shelf crashed to the floor, chairs toppled and Caesar O'Toole pitched against the bar, clutching his bottle of beer. Good thing the cooler's on solid ground, he thought. At least the beer's safe.

The tremor at Iscariot's was mild compared with the shock waves that hit Calvary. Actually, it was not a powerful earthquake. On a normal day, with few people about the state park at Calvary, the casualties would have been few. But today, with thousands of people packing the park to catch sight of Jesus' crucifixion, the devastation was magnified. The dam that held back the St. Joseph River could not withstand the force of the earthquake, and it split, dumping thousands of tons of water into the park. Culverts washed out. Automobiles were turned over, picked up, spun by the deluge as the river rushed its way toward Lake Michigan. People were picked up, spun around, washed hundreds of yards.

Half a mile from Calvary, a dark-haired woman with large breasts and three cameras dangling from parts of her body sat perched high in a pine tree.

"Damn!"

Directly below Carla, a little girl about nine or ten years old was pinned in a deep fissure the quake had rent in the landscape. Carla could not see what held the girl's leg, but rescuers had been unable to remove her. Slowly, water was creeping into the hole. It had started with the girl lying trapped in a mucky puddle in the hole. But half an hour later, the water had reached her waist. It was clear that nothing would stop the water, and that if she was not removed soon, she would drown.

Suddenly, a voice crackled over Carla's radio.

"Strumpff! Can you hear me?"

"Who's that?" shouted Carla.

The little girl looked up at the camerawoman in the tree. Her eyes spoke terror. They beseeched Carla for help.

"It's me, Caesar," the voice said. "I've set up a command post at Iscariot's Bar. What's going on?"

"What's going on? This assignment just turned into a Pulitzer, Caesar. I've got a little girl who's trapped with water seeping into this hole, and she's going to drown pretty soon unless somebody helps her. But the fire and police people are all concentrating on the crucifixion. They've split. I'm recording every stage of her tragedy. It's an incredible piece of luck!"

A steady-minded editor might have said to Carla, "Why aren't you at Calvary?" But Caesar instead bubbled, "Hey, fantastic! Stay with it. Over and out."

Carla frowned. A TV cameraman, spotting her in the tree, had come over to chat. He was standing at the edge of the hole, but at first didn't see the girl. He was engrossed in commenting to Carla that the crucifixion was behind schedule and Channel Two was forced to bump it from the five o'clock news.

"Now, with this goddam quake, the whole thing could be upstaged," the cameraman said.

Carla was in a quandary. She could see water gradually rising toward the girl's shoulders, but she didn't want to take a picture and alert TV that a human drama was unfolding at his feet.

Now, worse luck, Howard Waldorf, the portly News and Free Press reporter from that paper's Gethsemane office, had noticed the TV camera and was walking over for a look.

"Jesus H. Christ!" Carla swore. What rotten luck! Waldorf came right up to the tree and didn't even notice Carla. Dolt! Never even looked up. Instead, he took in the little girl's plight and departed.

"God, what a relief!" Carla said.

"What?" said the cameraman.

"Oh, nothing, I just had to shift my weight. It's no picnic sitting in this tree, I can tell you."

"Say, why are you crouched in that pine, anyway? You're a good half mile from the crosses."

Carla was saved from either an embarrassing admission or a bald-faced lie as Waldorf came back carrying a canteen. The chubby reporter squatted down and held the canteen by its strap, lowering it to the little girl.

That was too much for Carla, who could no longer contain herself now that the News and Free Press was directly meddling in her work.

"Hey, Waldorf! Don't you think that's a bit heavy?" shouted Carla. "Your job is to record, not give first aid. Besides, I can't get a clear shot with your fat ass in the way."

Through her telephoto lens, Carla could see the girl's eyes again trained on her. There was a dark anger in the girl's face, mixed with pain.

Carla's rage grew as she watched the TV man unscrew the lens cap from his video camera. Goddam! Now he's spotted the kid! This will be on the evening news!

"This kid's not going to last until the nightly news," said Waldorf, again walking away. "I'm going to find a pump and get that water out of there."

Carla could not believe her ears. Where the hell were that guy's ethics? Not to mention his deadline. A journalist was supposed to be objective, and here was Howard Waldorf getting involved, actually trying to change the course of events.

It was too much.

But then Carla had a second thought, if that is what it's called: The News and Free Press was always short on staff, and Howard was no doubt the only reporter they'd assigned to cover the crucifixion. With Waldorf hunting for a pump, the competition could kiss their cross coverage good-bye! Carla had to chuckle at that. Because TV and radio don't count, really — in one ear and out the other eye, no paper record and all.

So we've got an exclusive, after all!

As Carla climbed down from the tree and headed on foot toward Calvary Hill, Caesar O'Toole began writing his letter to the Pulitzer Prize Board at Columbia University to recommend the Filibuster's crucifixion coverage for the most coveted award in journalism.

Photographer Carla Strumpff and reporter Daley Strumm arrived in Calvary in the midst of an earthquake that killed thousands as Jesus Christ and two thieves were being crucified. To meet a deadline in faraway Detroit, they had less than an hour to capture the enormity of it all. The pictures and prose speak for themselves.

Carla Strumpff and Daley Strumm captured the pain, the agony, the distress and, finally, the quiet of a girl's death after an earthquake that accompanied the crucifixion of Jesus Christ, the most important event in history.

The focus of their work was the execution of the religious zealot, Jesus. To reach Calvary, Strumm drove a car that suffered a battery failure and a smashed rear window and that eventually collided with a ten-point deer. Along the way, through uncanny sleuthing ability, Strumm discovered the lair of the arch-traitor, Judas, and was nearby when that villain confessed privately and later hanged himself.

Strumpff meanwhile captured one of the most gripping photographs of the execution calamity by photographing the gradual drowning of ten-year-old Linda Bloom, trapped in earthquake debris, her leg pinned by a collapsed concrete slab. Her head was barely above water as one intrepid rescue worker sought to free her.

The next day, Bloom died from exposure and exhaustion after being trapped for fifty-four hours. Strumpff's pictures, which appeared on page one of the Filibuster, brought this terrible tragedy home to thousands of readers in Michigan. The pictures also served as a warning that public executions can be dangerous places.

O'Toole was moved nearly to tears by his own prose, and a thought crossed his mind: If we really do win a Pulitzer, we could even say that Linda Bloom's life was not lost in vain.

Indeed, then it could be said that the little girl gave up her life so that Carla Strumpff and Daley Strumm, with of course some mention of their editor, Caesar O'Toole, might win their Pulitzer.

chapter XXIII

THE BIG ONE

A long ribbon of yellow police tape twisted out of sight around the foot of Calvary Hill. It was a warning to spectators: Don't venture any nearer the crosses. Atop the hill, silhouettes of the three rough-hewn barn timbers thrust upward in off-kilter X shapes. But they could not be seen clearly enough to satisfy Carla Strumpff. However, the Filibuster photog had a problem. Every fifty feet, a state trooper armed with pistol and handie talkie stood ready to stop unauthorized people from trying to approach the scene of crucifixion.

At a break in the tape, Carla Strumpff spoke with a policeman.

"Public's not allowed near the scene of crucification," the cop said.

"I'm not the public," said Carla patiently. "I'm a photographer with the Detroit Filibuster."

"Filibuster, hey? Long way from home, aren't you?"

"My editors felt this was an important story, and they wanted me to record the event. The public has a right to know what goes on at these crucifixions. Now, if you don't mind, I'm working against a tight deadline and need to get closer."

"Yeah, sure. Funny the way this one's drawn you guys' attention. We crucitize guys every other day at Calvary and normally you never see the news media."

"Well, here I am — I need to get past you."

"Let's see some proof of who or whom you are."

Carla set her big brown canvas bag on the ground and unzipped the flap. She pulled out a stack of plastic-coated identification cards and handed them to the officer.

"Hmmm, Carla Strumm," the trooper murmured. "Hmmm." He held his handie talkie to his face and said, "Hey, Chet, don't we have a bulletin on someone named Strumm?"

"Yeah," a voice came through the little radio. "We're supposed to arrest him on sight."

"This is a her."

"Well, maybe it's a gal. All I know is Pilate wants Strumm detained. He's not supposed to get near the crucifaction."

"My name isn't Strumm," Carla said. "It's Strumpff. Pfffff!"

"Pfffff, yourself, lady. Don't split hairs with me," the cop said. "Strumm or Strumpff, it's all the same. You don't get near the crucifactory. Come along with me." Holding her elbow tight, the policeman pushed Carla toward a deep blue squad car.

"I told you, I'm Strumpff! I'm not Strumm. You want Daley Strumm, not me!"

"It's close enough. You're under arrest, Honey. Don't make this difficult."

"Jesus Christ!" screamed Carla. "You cops are all alike — you can't spell!"

Now, a person given to reading tea leaves might divine some great, even cosmic, significance from Carla Strumpff's arrest and detention. Might even propose that it was ordained by powers on high, by which I mean heavenly authority, that the Filibuster not take pictures of the crucifixion. But since television was shooting pictures throughout and the good old News and Free Press guy had chosen to canter down some humanitarian sidetrack, such an interpretation would seem to impute discrimination specifically against the Filibuster to those powers that ordain what will and what will not be. From a cosmic perspective, hardly fair, it would seem.

Or someone with a tendency toward discovering great significance in obscure minutiae might even say the name confusion itself was meaningful: that Strumpff was sacrificed so that Strumm might pass through the gates and perform some divinely reasoned-out task at the crucifixion.

However, that would prove to be a hasty guess.

First, because it hardly seems fair to blame the blundering excesses of the Detroit Filibuster on God.

And second, because as Daley Strumm pulled the red and rather beat-up Filibuster station wagon slowly across the grass at the foot of Calvary Hill, he too was stopped by a state trooper.

"You're under arrest, buddy," the cop said.

"What?" blinked Daley Strumm. "What for?" Suddenly he remembered Judas swaying under the water pipe and panicked. Did somebody suspect that he'd murdered Iscariot?

"W-what's this all about?" Daley stammered.

"Don't play dumb, pal. I can see that poor deer on the floor back there. Jesus Christ, what a callous son of a bitch you news guys are. You hit the deer, smash your windshield all to hell, then drive around with the animal half dead in the back of your wagon. What if that buck kicked the bucket? You're gonna let all that good venison spoil? You could at least have put the animal out of its misery."

The trooper swung the car's back hatch open and yelled, "Hey, Chet! Look at this! Ten point rack on this thing!"

Suddenly, the deer was up and bounding out the back door, bowling the trooper onto his back. Casually, the buck loped across the grass while the policeman stood up and brushed off the seat of his pants.

Turning to Daley, he said, "You're under arrest, buddy."

"On what charge?" asked Daley.

"To begin with, obstructing a police officer."

"How did I obstruct you? It was the deer that knocked you down."

"It doesn't matter. That's not the big one, anyway."

"The big what?"

"Big charge." The cop grinned.

"What's the big charge?"

"Cruelty to an animal."

chapter XXIV

A LITTLE SWITCHEROO

In the squad car, on the way to the Gethsemane lockup, trooper Barney Clawson lectured Daley Strumm on the evils of wasting good venison.

"I wouldn't of took you in at all if I'd a thought that meat would be put to good use," the trooper said.

"But the deer wasn't even dead — it got away," said Daley.

"That's what I mean. Waste of good venison."

Daley couldn't understand the policeman's logic, and gave up arguing. Obviously, he wasn't going to talk his way out of jail. Not with this cop. He'd have to wait till he saw a judge. At some point, fairly soon, they'd have to arraign him and set bond. Then he'd tell his story to a judge — a rational, educated person — and be set free. Probably without even being charged.

But Trooper Clawson wasn't about to give up on the conversation. It wasn't every day that a state trooper in the western boondocks of Michigan got to arrest a reporter from the Detroit Filibuster. The trooper desperately needed some good morsel of inside gossip or some freak happening that he could take away from this encounter and use to regale his buddies at the state police post, at coffee hour after temple or in the Elks bar.

Like a barber angling for a tip by projecting conviviality, this copper also felt it part of his duty to cultivate his captive in a friendly way. Lots of times when you were detaining someone they would take it personally, like it was you, the cop, who was wrecking their life by putting them in jail. When really it was just the requirement of the job, and if it wasn't Trooper Clawson turning the key and throwing it away, some other police type would be doing it. Might as well resign yourself to what lay ahead and pass the time of day with a friendly flatfoot.

Besides, there was always the chance that Clawson's goodwill would pay off by eliciting a freewill confession of some immense crime Daley had committed and thus seal the trooper's promotion to corporal. That's why, surreptitiously, Clawson had turned a small cassette tape recorder on as he entered the squad car.

"So you're a reporter on the Filibuster," the trooper said.

"Uh-huh," said Daley.

"That's the big time in your field, I guess," Trooper Clawson said. "I mean, you don't get much bigger than the Filibuster."

"Oh, everything is relative," said Daley.

"All the same, you're sure a heck of a lot bigger than our little Argus-Palladium. Boy, there's a crew for you. Rinky-dink? We call it the 'Gargle Palace.' My God, the things they print supposedly as news. They give the rest of you journalists a bad name, I tell you. We don't hesitate to nip them in the bud whenever we can."

"Nip?"

"Oh, don't worry, we wouldn't pull that on anybody from out of town, unless they deserved it. Sure, they call in and we put them on hold for half an hour. So they send some green cub reporter over to get the news in person and we leave him cooling his heels and read it over the phone to the TV guys. They bug us, we bug them. You wouldn't have that sort of nonsense in Detroit, I don't think. In the big game, nobody's got time for that kind of crap."

Daley wasn't listening. Gradually the shock of being arrested and headed for jail had worn off and he'd begun thinking: How can they arrest me without a scrap of evidence?

"Hey, officer," Daley said, "I'm wondering. You're bringing me in on an animal cruelty charge, but the deer ran away. You don't have any proof."

"Oh, sure we do," Trooper Clawson said. He reached toward the dashboard and picked up a microphone. "Six-two to one-one-four: you read me, Red?"

"Loud and clear."

"Any luck on the deer patrol?"

Over the radio, a voice said, "Hey, Claws, great luck! Ten points in the cooler, gutted and waiting for the butcher. You take the south half, I'll take the north."

Trooper Clawson chuckled at his comrade's joke.

"You killed it!" shouted Daley Strumm.

"Had to," said Trooper Clawson. "For its own good. No telling what kind of internal injuries it sustained when you crashed into it. We saved it from dying miserably in some flea-ridden swamp."

Now, Trooper Clawson had taken a nearly instant liking to Daley as the two were riding in the patrol car, but he was beginning to have second thoughts about the reporter. The guy seemed awfully rigid. In fact, that was his impression generally of newspeople. They tended to hold others to awfully high standards, yet who was holding them to any standards? Nobody. They could slam you in print and you couldn't touch them — in print, that is. But there were other ways, off the pages of daily newspapers, where a smart policeman could find revenge.

Like dumping them in the Gethsemane slammer and throwing away the key! Talk about a tale to tell. Hah! Trooper Clawson couldn't wait to get to the Elks and regale his pals about how there's one way to censor the news: Put the reporters in the crapper.

Daley Strumm would find the Gethsemane lockup a foul enough place, crammed with drunken humanity hauled away from the crucifixion. The execution still had not begun, and revelers were becoming angry and drunk, drunk and angry, and were posing quite a problem to the police assigned to keep order at the foot of Calvary. And that damned earthquake hadn't lessened the cops' problems any. The worst thing, of course, was these snooping reporters — although there were some benefits even there. For instance, a photogenic cop or one with a good gift of gab might hope to inveigle a television reporter into putting his mug on the evening news for family and friends to gawk at. There was near-instant gratification in that. If your wife was alert, she'd snatch a copy with the video recorder so you could play and replay your ten seconds of electronic glory at the Elks or over at the volunteer fire department when you got off duty.

The lockup door with its solid steel bars clanged shut behind Daley Strumm, and he blinked in the dim light shed by the caged twenty-five-watt bulb mounted high on the ceiling. He could make out dark, horizontal forms on steel bunks with no mattresses. On the floor he could see more of these elongated lumps. Somehow, the mass of humanity incarcerated here had found a way to sleep it off.

Meanwhile, the cops had taken his pen, notebook, belt and watch.

"That's so you can't hang yourself!"

The odor of urine and sweat reeked in the still air of the cell.

"Barabbas!" a jailer stuck his head around a corner and yelled into the cell. "Barabbas!"

A glum-looking man in his early twenties flinched each time the name was called. He was sitting cross-legged in a far corner of the cell, staring at the floor. At the third call of "Barabbas!" the man started to stand up.

"Wait a minute, don't get up," the jailer said. "Just checking. We may need you in a minute."

"What's going on?" asked Strumm.

The jailer, a skinny man with a beer belly, looked Daley over, then seemed to recognize him.

"Oh yeah, you're the Filibuster guy. Ain't often we get celebrities in here. That guy's Barabbas, and we may pull a little switcheroo in a minute. Little shell game, know what I mean? Depending on how our telephone survey goes, we may stick Barabbas on the cross instead of Jesus."

"You mean this guy may be executed?"

"Maybe. And maybe Jesus won't be. All depends on the will of the people. This is a democratic country, you know."

Once again, Daley realized, he was at the center of the story of Jesus' crucifixion. He felt tremendous pity for this man, Barabbas, who might be chosen to die in place of Jesus. Incredible! This was a major chunk of the story! He looked at the man sitting on the floor and felt awe. How could he possibly approach a man who was in such a state and conduct an interview? The Filibuster's errand seemed so petty, pointless, futile.

Of course, if he didn't interview Barabbas, he would have to tell nobody, absolutely nobody, at the Filibuster, about this chance encounter. Otherwise, he would be severely reprimanded for incompetence, if not fired — or worse, sent to the Gethsemane Bureau. Failing to interview a key subject on a story as important as this, no matter if it was for reasons of conscience, was like filling out an application to cover night cops.

But how could he possibly intrude on what might well be Barabbas' last moments alive?

"You work for the Filibuster?"

The words floated across the cell, cutting through Daley's reverie. He looked up. It was Barabbas, talking to him.

"Yes," said Daley.

"What are you in here for?"

"Cruelty to a deer. But it's not true."

"I know, I know; We're all innocent in here. You don't need to explain. Smoke? Want a cigarette? God, what a jam I got myself into this time."

"What kind of a jam?" Daley asked.

"You really want to hear?"

"It's my job to listen, if you don't mind."

"Well, if you listen to me, you'll be the first. I know, Jesus is probably saying the same thing. They've got him in isolation upstairs."

"So why are you in here?"

"Not because I'm innocent, I can tell you that. You really want to hear my story?"

"Why not?" said Daley. "It's something to do. Are we on or off the record?"

"Well, so my friends will know my story — on."

Daley concentrated. He would have to remember well everything Barabbas said, because there was no pen, no paper — only his memory to write on.

chapter XXV

JUDGE BANG-BANG

Daley Strumm was dozing, stretched on one of the steel bunks. His shoulders hurt, his back hurt; there was no comfortable way to lie on such a hard surface. Here is the nightmare that he dreamed as he lay in that cell. It was not the first time Daley had dreamed this, but it came only when he was in the middle of an important reporting assignment at the Filibuster.

Somehow, Daley is present in the newsroom without anyone there knowing it. The dayside people are all gone. Nightside — they are the shadowy ghosts who shepherd the newspaper into print after all the big-name columnists, writers, editors and dozens of petty hacks and errand people have gone home to bed. To readers, these people are nobodies — their bylines never appear in the paper. Even to staffers, they are non-entities. Unknown, faceless people whose voices they sometimes contact by telephone. But these are the people with real power at the paper. Every word that goes to the presses must receive their approval.

It is several hours since Daley has filed a big story, a project he has worked on for months. He has battled with dayside editors to make sure there is agreement on every sentence in his report. He has been assured the story will play on page one the next day, and it is to run at full length — a long thirty-five inches of news copy. The story, in fact, has been held for several weeks in anticipation of a slow news day when space would be available for a controversial religion story.

Now, according to his dream, he secretly patrols the newsroom as a skeleton night crew readies the paper for printing. There is a night editor, a rewrite man, a copy editor. A triumvirate holding absolute power over the contents of tomorrow's paper.

Unseen, Daley stands near Gordon Long, nightside editor. The telephone rings.

"Detroit Filibuster," Long says.

Seconds later, Long cups his hand over the telephone microphone and yells at Will Barrett, rewrite man: "It's Daley Strumm. He wants to make sure we didn't cut his story."

"Which story is that?" Barrett, a thin, wispy man, asks in a clear, slow baritone.

"It's I-TEMPLE-XIX."

"Well, it's on the budget for IA tomorrow," says Barrett.

"It's on the budget for IA tomorrow," repeats Long into the phone. Seconds later, he hangs up.

"How did Strumm want that story?" Barrett asked.

"He wanted to know where it was going," said Long.

"No, not 'What did he want?' I said, 'How did he want it?' How did he come across?"

"Oh, I see, Will. I forgot, you're in the P-slot tonight. Let me think. Well, he came across as suspicious. I think he thought maybe we spiked his story."

"Are you kidding? That's a lot of nerve, Gordie. He has no right suspecting you of tampering with his story."

The telephone rang again. Again Long answered. "Detroit Filibuster."

Long listened for a minute, then said, "Space is always a problem. Always. We're trying to get it in, but it's not our only concern here tonight. We've got the entire paper to nail down." Again he hung up.

"Strumm again."

"Two calls within five minutes? Where's he coming from? He's got no business hassling you that way, Gordie. I'm assessing a six-G deficit for the first call and another six-Gs for the second call. We'll see how he likes having twelve paragraphs lopped off the end of his story!"

"I don't agree with that, Will."

"You don't? But he sassed you, as good as smarted-off to you, implying that anyone from nightside would mess with his holier-than-thou copy."

"Oh, I'm not saying we shouldn't assess Punishment. I just don't see why we necessarily have to cut the twelve-G penalty off the end of his story. We've got the time to be more creative than that! Why not pull it out of the middle, or even amputate his lead?"

"Now we're cookin'. Hey, tell me, Gordie; am I mistaken, or did I see Peg Morris rush by you tonight without saying hello?"

"She did. She was in a hurry to get to an interview. She usually greets me fine."

"All the same, I'm assessing five Gs against that story she wrote."

"You'll have a hard time doing that — I already trimmed it down to four grafs."

Well, then, that's simple." Will hit a few keys on his computer terminal. "There! Spiked the story out completely."

"You don't have to say 'completely,'" chuckled Long. "If you spike it, the whole thing's gone. No sense in nightside doing overkill. 'No redundancy,' that's our motto."

A few minutes later, Long frowned. "You know, short as it was, or short as we made it, that Morris story is on the budget, and somebody's bound to ask questions tomorrow."

"Hell, just give them the old 'no space' line, Gordie. If any of those daysiders ever actually worked nights they'd find out fast what a crock that 'no space' yarn is, but in twenty-three years at rewrite, I've never once had anyone challenge me."

"You know," added Will, "you get on my case for being harsh with these reporters, and by extension, their daytime editors. But I think I'm really pretty lenient. Certainly I don't go as far as old Ralph Ott. God! Now there was a rewrite man with a vengeance. A dayside reporter would piss Ralph off. Ralph disappears for a few minutes, comes back and leans over the reporter's shoulder. Makes the "T" sign with his hands and hisses, 'Four-T! Four-T!' Few hours later, reporter gets off work and goes to his car. Finds all four tires slashed. 'Four-T! Four-T!' But you know what? Being reporters, not one of them ever made the connection."

The near-empty newsroom filled with the roar of laughter from these two nighttime staffers.

Daley Strumm stirred uneasily. As he woke, the nightmare receded. Now, he sensed that something in the cell had changed. The other inmates, including Barabbas, were asleep. But somebody else was in this stinky, barred room. Somebody who had not been here earlier. Daley could not recall hearing the cell door open. He was lying with his head a few inches from the hinge side of the door and would have roused if anyone had been brought in.

He sensed, rather than saw, someone moving quietly but purposefully close to him. Daley opened his eyes. A gaunt man with high cheekbones, close-cut curly hair and a short but full beard was kneeling beside him. Later, Daley remembered thinking: His hair is supposed to be long and flowing in gentle curls. But that was not the case.

Daley looked into the man's eyes. At the same time, strangely, he was no longer aware of the aches in his shoulders and back. He felt peaceful, all of a sudden at one with himself. He was sure he knew who this man was, and found it odd that this man's eyes were twinkling. There was something humorous in those eyes, and there was also something that gave Daley a glowing feeling — the feeling he had had since childhood of well-being, of physical warmth, when someone had treated him kindly.

This man who seemed to create unusual emotional side effects in people around him leaned over and whispered to Daley, "You don't need to worry. My story is the world's story, and it will become known regardless of what happens to you or what your newspaper does with it. Be careful and take care of yourself."

Suddenly, the stranger was gone. Daley fell sound asleep. When he awoke some time later, he could not tell how much time had passed and he could not distinguish the real from the dream.

He recalled the P-men, and in the first blinking seconds of wakefulness actually believed he lived in a real world where nighttime employees of the Filibuster exacted arbitrary punishments against their colleagues for imaginary infractions.

The same old dream, he suddenly realized.

What about that mysterious visitor? That was not the same old dream.

Bang!

The sound of a gunshot echoed through the building.

Bang!

Daley had jumped off the bench at the first shot.

"Don't get excited," Barabbas laughed. "That's only Judge Bang-Bang."

"Who's Judge Bang-Bang?" Daley asked.

"Oh, his real name is Judge Bannon, but everybody calls him Judge Bang-Bang. He's nuts. He's afraid some criminal he sentenced is going to come back and assassinate him. He's got a bulletproof bench, but he doesn't trust it. Every night he sneaks back into the court and checks. Unloads a revolver at it."

So much for finding a decent, rational, educated person to hear my case, thought Daley in despair.

But was Judge Bang-Bang also a dream? Was this whole situation, this assignment, just a nightmare from which he would awaken?

"Hey, Daley," said Barabbas. "Notice anything different about this place?"

Daley looked all around and saw that he and Barabbas were the only people left in the cell.

"Where did the others go?"

"Jailbreak," said Barabbas.

"How?"

"Well, the crucifixion was about to start. I won the survey, by the way, so it's Jesus they're going to nail up. Anyway, this cop comes in, says they're all supposed to be at Calvary. State law won't allow them to leave locked-up prisoners unattended. What if the place burns down, you know? 'Yer on yer honor, assholes!' this cop yells, and leaves the door unlocked. Now, each of us has to make his own decision about whether to stay or go. I've made my decision — I don't trust those donkeys not to nail me up at a later date, so it's hors d'oeuvre for now, happy trails, and nice to meet you."

"Au revoir, you mean," corrected Daley.

Barabbas walked out.

Now the cell was vacant except for Daley Strumm. The honor system had emptied the jail. What should he, a moral person, do?

Daley did not hesitate.

He laughed, trotting past the booking desk and pushing open the glass doors of the state police post.

"Hors d'oeuvre!"

In a parking lot he found the red Filibuster station wagon with the keys in the ignition. Now to get to Calvary, he thought. Finally I can accomplish my mission.

chapter XXVI

BOOK THE LEARJET

Chutney Vipes sat in front of the computer screen scanning the wire service news. He read the Amalgamated Press report. Reflexively, a headline formed in his mind: "Earthquake hampers, can't stop, crucifixion at Calvary."

"Hey, Don!" Vipes piped across the newsroom. "Maybe this explains why nothing from our crew at Calvary. They've had a quake out there. Long-distance lines are down."

"Anybody maimed or killed?" Strodum shouted back.

"Let's see," said Vipes, as he scanned the text. "Lots of people hurt, hundreds of buildings damaged, but only one or two deaths confirmed. And some kid trapped in a culvert. Expected to drown."

"Well, we've got a dozen dead now confirmed at our plane wreck, so that's still the lead for page one. Kid in the culvert sounds like a good story. Too bad it's not in Detroit — nobody gives a shit about out-state," Strodum said.

"Yeah, I'm inclined to make the quake a dateline, especially since we're not covering the crucifixion anyway."

"Except that until we get ahold of O'Toole and Strumm and Strumpff — we still are covering it," Strodum said.

"Correction." Chutney chuckled. "Covering it, but not running it." The city editor smiled. With the ordeal of the forced confession behind him, he reflected, he was starting to come back into form, be his usual self, a witty, carefree, fun guy. "Just another day in the mines, except now, with the phones knocked out, somebody's got to run out to Gethsemane and haul those folks back before they eat up thousands of solid gold buckos on expense account."

"I don't think you need to worry — O'Toole and Strumm have families. As soon as they're finished, they'll be heading straight home. They don't like motels."

"I'm not worried about them. Who cares about them? Remember, Strumm is expendable, and so — to be truthful — is Caesar. Hell, Don, my worry is Carla. Cost is no object to her, and she's probably already bivouacked in the Ritz. You know, when she covered the Republican convention, she racked up an $MMMMMMMM-hotel bill and leased a Rolls-Royce. Said it helped the GOP remember her. No, I'm afraid somebody's got to go out there and jerk their chain in person, and it can't be me."

"Why not?"

"Because, uh. . . " Vipes was not a rapid thinker, but one thing was sure: He knew it wouldn't do for Don to know that he had another date with Minky at the Chop House.

"So then it's settled," Chut said, hopping over an embarrassing pause as if it were a mere crack in the floor. "You'll take a company car and head out there, pronto."

Strodum was a quick thinker, and he'd already seen this coming. What worked for Caesar ought to work for the gander, he thought. "Don't forget, I've got kids, too, Chut," Strodum said.

"Hey, take them along! Give them an outing and expense off your meals and gas."

"Take my family to a crucifixion? Are you nuts?"

"Well, don't take them, then — it's all the same to me. But get moving now, hubba-hubba, chop-chop!"

"This means I'll have to stop at the Gethsemane Bureau, doesn't it?"

"Afraid so, Don."

Strodum found the prospect of visiting the Gethsemane Bureau unpleasant for a reason that was clear and well-defined. It was legend among Filibuster staff that the paper's most sarcastic malcontents had been banished to that remote office where their faces no longer had to be part of a newsroom scene which, God knows, was vicious enough without them.

Out in the far-off wasteland of the Gethsemane Bureau these crea-tures were intended to languish, half-forgotten. Their names certainly never popped up in those daily planning meetings that were so all-im-portant to furthering careers. They were left with little to do other than practice imitations of David Caninski or write clandestine manuals on how to blackmail management into handing over long periods of va-cation time in return for alleged long periods of overtime supposedly worked.

Compensatory time was the name of the game in Gethsemane, and the formula, one-point-five times N, where N was a fantasy about hours of OT worked, was the subject of this surreptitious handbook known by the title of "Mine Comp."

Yes, there was a soft-boiled insurrection going on out in Gethsemane, and Strodum knew he was a target of much of these half-baked rebels' jibes and vitriol-hurling. It was one thing to deal with these numbskulls over the telephone. But to meet them face-to-face on their home turf was a specter that made Strodum's belly heave.

Take his kids out there, indeed! Expense account? Hmmm. Strodum smiled as he checked his wallet. Yes, MasterCard and Visa are in place.

Looking through a copy of the Detroit Yellow Pages, he found what he wanted: a charter air service based at Detroit's Metro Airport.

Strodum punched in the number.

"This is Don Strodum, deputy city editor at the Filibuster. I need to charter a plane immediately for Gethsemane General Airport."

"Certainly, Mr. Strodum. We have available right now a Piper Az-tec. That's a twin piston-engine plane and would make the trip in about an hour, give or take, depending on headwinds. Or, we have a Learjet, which is considerably faster but also considerably more expensive."

"Book the Learjet. Put it on the Filibuster account. Warn the pilot I'll want him to wait for me when we get there. No idea how long I'll be."

One more family man headed for the crucifixion, Strodum thought wryly.

Onward to Calvary!

chapter XXVII

A MOST PRESTIGIOUS MORON

One floor above the newsroom, David Caninski leaned back in his leather chair and frowned at the man sitting on the opposite side of his desk.

It was no use. Frowns didn't budge Herod, King of Detroit.

"I'll repeat myself — again," said Herod. "It is perfectly possible for our police to release your star columnist. At this point, no other media outlets know we've got him on a whoring charge. That won't last long. Rumors already are floating out of the department. I can stop all that by placing him back in your hands. All I'm asking is that you promise me this newspaper's full, immediate and complete endorsement in next year's monarchical election. And, of course, I want your promise in writing. That way" — Herod chuckled — "if you renege, I've got your John Hancock to blackmail you with."

Dopey use of a preposition, thought Caninski, but he held his tongue. No use getting Herod all riled up about something trivial.

"You would ask us duh to compromise our integrity?" Caninski was furious, not at the nature of the request, for it was not unknown for the Filibuster to barter editorial endorsements. No, he was furious to find himself, personally, in Herod's grasp.

"Our loyal Filibuster readers duh believe in this newspaper, Herod. This newspaper is considered duh incorruptible, unlike a duh certain city government. What do you think would happen to this duh institution's reputation for credibility if word of this deal you're proposing leaked out?"

"You ain't got no credibility to lose, Dave."

Furious, Caninski stared at Herod. This insulting magnate thought he could sit here and blackmail the publisher of the Detroit Filibuster. And he was right! He could blackmail Caninski. But this was more than business now. This was personal. Caninski struggled to control himself, however. Keep your sights duh on the immediate objective and duh forget the indignities this half-witted potentate is dishing out.

"Okay," said Caninski. "You win, Herod. But I want a clause in this contract that says the entire deal is secret."

"Sure. But I want a clause that says the first fawning, pro-Herod editorial gets written today and published Saturday — that's tomorrow."

What a dope, thought Caninski. This monarchical monkey is duh so dense he doesn't know we sell fewer papers on Saturday than any duh other day. So much for Herod's vaunted duh shrewdness. He's getting the worst duh of this bargain!

"You win duh Herod," Caninski repeated.

Herod, a rotund man with thick, gray-black sideburns and a spherical nose, leaned back, drew a Havana cigar from the breast pocket of his suit coat and lit it with a butane lighter that emitted a flame like a blowtorch. It occurred to Caninski that he had fired Filibuster staffers for violating his ban on smoking in company buildings. He wished he could fire Herod.

As the king exhaled a long billow of blue smoke, he caught sight of the newly framed Caninski motto hanging behind and above the publisher's head. Herod read the motto and read it again to make sure he hadn't made a mistake. No, he had read correctly. But now, in a typical move of overconfidence, Herod made a grievous tactical error.

"Why Dave, you sly old hypocrite, you! All those pious Sunday columns about the sanctity of family. Ha-ha! You old coxswain, you!"

"What in the world duh are you running on about now, Herod?"

"Why, Dave, that sign up there — hell, Dave, that sounds like something I would have said. 'I've never had two bad lays in a row.' Damn, Dave, I wish I *had* said that!"

Furious now, Caninski went over the edge. "You damned illiterate fool, Herod, duh who the hell ever taught you to read? What am I duh doing sitting here discussing business with you, the city's most duh prestigious moron? What the duh hell are you talking about?"

Caninski turned, sensing as he did so that by reacting in any way to Herod's ribbing he was losing dignity. Then he took in the new sign and realized that — goddam! — Herod was right! It in fact did now read to the effect that he had never had two negative sexual encounters seriatim.

Caninski's fury was so great that he forgot about Mutt Prescott. Forgot about the deal with Herod, the contract, the bought-and-paid-for editorial endorsements.

"You slimy bastard! You get out of my duh office. I never want to see you again, you duh municipal creep! You civic worm! You, Herod, are a duh turd in the gut of the body politic, a giant duh slug in the garden of government! God damn, Herod, I've waited a duh long time to tell you how I feel, and now I duh am about to say it. You are a disgusting duh venal duh revolting duh heap of dross. A political pit viper. Out! Duh, out of my office, out of my duh newspaper. Out! Out! Duh, out!"

Herod, followed by scampering police bodyguards, scurried out of the publisher's office. Caninski calmed himself down and tried to think rationally about his next step.

Herod still had Mutt Prescott, and now, having failed to play him as a hostage, could be expected to lay him on the table, a royal flush. There would be instant leaks to the News and Free Press, WWJ, channels Two, Four and Seven. Channel Fifty would pick it off the wire and Fifty-six, the public station, would wait a few days, then convene a panel of journalists and politicians to discuss the long-term implications. Meanwhile, Mutt's mug would be on the eleven o'clock news, along with the disclosure — Herod had informed Dave of this — that the Filibuster had been paying for Mutt's sessions with prostitutes for the last five years. The damned fool had expensed off the prostitutes' fees!

Two reporters, one from Amalgamated Print and the other from the New Imperial Times, happened to be passing the publisher's office on their way back to cramped offices in the Filibuster subbasement. Both would later confirm each other's report that they heard a scream come from Caninski's office.

"God! How many whores have we paid?"

These two sets of roving eyes and ears could not see Caninski slump into his chair, then suddenly sit stiffly upright. But they heard the loud groan, followed by the exclamation, "I've never had two bad lays in a row!"

God only knew what Herod would do with that choice nugget! But the Times and AP knew what to do with it.

Caninski jumped out of his chair, swung round and grabbed the framed motto. He tried to wedge his fingers behind the cardboard backing and the nails that held the paper and glass in place. But Graphics had done a thorough job of tightening this frame. Finally, exasperated, he smashed the glass against a corner of his desk, pulled the motto out, tore it up, grabbed the fragments of paper and rushed to his private washroom.

The sound of a commode being flushed continued on and off for five minutes.

"Herod can't leak that to the press — he can't prove it. I'll deny it. I'll sue his ass off. He doesn't have a copy. He's dead in the water."

Now to get down to business. Any minute now, WWJ and WJR would break into regular programming to flash the news that Mutt was in the slammer. But once that came out, Herod would have played his hand.

The Filibuster needed to fix up an apologetic, nonexplanatory story about Mutt, quick, for tomorrow's paper. Those hacks on the third floor could do that easily enough.

What Caninski needed now was a little time to think over his countermove. Herod had declared war on him. On the Filibuster. An institution that had been in Detroit far longer than the sham democratic monarchy known as the House of Herod.

Jesus H. Christ, Caninski thought. This is a royal mess. Wait a minute! That's it: Jesus Christ! Caninski grinned for the first time on this ugly Friday in April and began unconsciously rubbing his hands. Ha-ha! That's it! Ponty wanted our crucifixion coverage stifled as a favor to help him with Herod. Herod is the one who ordered Jesus crucified.

If only there were a way to save Jesus from the cross. Hey, that would spoil Herod's fun, wouldn't it? But at this late date, there was no way the paper could meddle behind the scenes to try to alter the course of history.

But hot damn! There is something we can do. Hell, we're a newspaper after all, aren't we? Hey, Herod doesn't want publicity for this thing, screw him. We'll cover every last square inch of that cross! It's not too late to fly somebody out there, even now.

Caninski sat down at his computer screen and logged on. He wrote "MSG VIPES" and told Chutney, electronically, "Put every available reporter from every department on the crucifixion story. Pronto. Play it top of One in tomorrow's paper."

Caninski pushed the SEND key and, having initiated that piece of skulduggery to his satisfaction, decided he was much more comfortable with himself.

Far better anyway than giving in to Herod's blackmail, he thought. His temper, he congratulated himself, had saved him from committing an ethical breach of monstrous proportions.

Unfortunately, Chutney Vipes was not near a computer terminal and therefore could not read his boss's latest edict.

Vipes was stepping off an elevator in the Filibuster lobby as Caninski was pressing the SEND key on his terminal. Vipes saw Minky reading something on a bulletin board and chuckling.

Chut stood beside her and read the sign, a photocopy of a motto that said, "I've never had two bad lays in a row. David Caninski."

"I saw that on the newsroom bulletin board," Chut said.

"It's all over the building," Minky said.

"Harmless fun," Chut said. "Chop House, Pancho?"

"Let's went, Cisco." Minky laughed.

chapter XXVIII

FUN'S OVER

Calvary State Park is a rolling meadow shaded by large oak and maple trees, with slow-moving Calvary Creek winding through one of the state's finest picnic grounds. At the center of this park stands Calvary Hill, a blunt knob where, in happier times, couples went to sit on benches and gaze at the sun as it set in amber, red and orange hues over Lake Michigan. By order of both Herod and Pilate, the benches have been removed so that on state-ordered occasions heavy timbers can be erected for executing the government's most despised criminals.

Wild horses could not have kept the public from viewing the killing of Jesus and his side-mates, the two thieves. But an earthquake, combined with sporadic power outages, water-main ruptures, natural-gas leaks and a medley of flooded basements had forced many people to look after their own needs and leave executing despised persons to the state.

Still, there were knots of onlookers as Daley Strumm parked the beleaguered Filibuster station wagon on the gravel lot and hiked through the park. We could best sum up Daley's mental state as numbness, a mixture of exhaustion enhanced by the aches of jail cell slumber and driven by his professional need to accomplish what he had been assigned to do: his job.

Daley tried not to think very deeply about the past twenty-four hours. His life had turned into a real dung heap. Bad, bad luck. About the only decent thing that had happened was the cops' mistaking Carla Strumpff for Daley and arresting her. Even that bit of foolishness gave him some cause for anxiety — guilt, rather — at the thought that another person was being punished in his place.

But punished for what? And of course, there was this other factor. Daley didn't want to think too hard about this because it wasn't pleasant admitting it. He didn't like Carla, considered her a crawling, slimy, two-faced wretch who would do anything short of murder for a photo and who justified the worst travesties by her universal dictum: The public has a right to see my pictures, regardless of how I take them. Therefore, he could not summon up a normal quota of sympathy for the photographer.

And what about those scenes with Barabbas and the mysterious stranger in jail? Were they real? Daley wasn't sure. Were these memories mere dreams assailing his uneasy lockup sleep?

Of course they were real! Every part had to be real, or the whole thing was a dream. And Daley had the muscle pains to remind him that his arrest had been the real McCoy. If one part was true, it was all true.

His memory backed up to an image of those three crossed beams. Those silhouettes, with the contorted human cargoes, lay etched in his mind. Now, as he approached again the hill where he planned to observe Jesus being slowly tortured to death, he reflected on this assignment that had ordered him to objectively record for the breakfast entertainment of Filibuster readers the agonies of a religious man condemned to die for his belief that there was good in human beings.

Suddenly that thought loomed largest, even larger than the assignment of reporting this horrible event. Daley's mind focused, not on the mechanics, logistics and politics of getting to the scene and doing the task, but on what he was supposed to see and report.

It was as if light flashed across his consciousness. This man is being killed — killed by other men who don't like what he believes. My God, thought Daley, this fate could fall on anyone — anyone who simply expresses an idea the authorities don't like.

If this can happen to Jesus, it can happen to me, to my wife, my kids — to anyone I know. Suddenly, Daley realized that he must get to the scene of crucifixion — not for the Filibuster, not for writing a news story, but so that he could relate this gruesome truth to his wife, to his young sons, to Wolfman. Yes, to Wolfman, who in his farseeing vision must have known that a time would come when Daley would no longer be driven by the Filibuster, but by his own need to know and pass on the knowledge.

Walking toward the hill, Daley had not been able to see the crosses. It was dark now, but there were streetlights on top of the hill. The cross silhouettes he had seen just before he was arrested were not visible. As he arrived at the line of yellow police tape, he still couldn't see the crosses.

A state trooper stood guard at the foot of the hill.

"What's going on? Why can't I see the crosses?" Daley asked.

"Fun's over," the trooper said. "Crosses came down an hour ago when the condemned expired."

"I'm too late?"

"Nah." The trooper laughed. "Wait for it to come 'round on video."

"I can't believe this! I'm sent all the way out here to cover this thing, and when I get here, it's over!"

If numb described Daley earlier, he could now be described as rigid, paralyzed. *Too late?*

"Excuse me, may I have a word with you?" said a slightly built young man with barely a hint of beard. "Please," he said, "step over here."

Daley did as he was told, moving out of earshot of the policeman.

"Are you Daley Strumm of the Filibuster?"

Daley was immediately suspicious. If this guy was a plainclothes cop, he might know the reporter was a fugitive from the police lockup.

"Yes," Daley reluctantly admitted. "That's who I am all right."

"My name is John. I talked with your editor, Caesar O'Toole. He thinks I'm a geek. Actually, I'm a follower of Jesus, and I was here during the crucifixion. I took notes, and you're welcome to use them if you like."

"Let's go," said Daley. "The Filibuster has a bureau near this place. You can come back there and help me write the story."

"Wonderful!" said John. "It's important that we start getting the Word out soon."

chapter XXIX

SPIKEROO

A thin man with gray hair parted in the middle and a pale face eases past Chutney Vipes and slides into a seat before a video terminal. Chutney pays no attention to Will Barrett, the nightside rewrite man. Nightside was a weird bunch; it didn't pay to get close to them.

None of the crew he sent to Calvary has reported back. Not knowing that Don Strodum has departed by Learjet, Chutney assumes his chief lieutenant is still on the highway aimed at Gethsemane and the dissident bureau there. He assumes it will be some hours yet before Strodum reports. With the crucifixion coverage long ago canceled, it doesn't matter that Strumpff, O'Toole and Strumm have not called.

It is evening, and Chutney, accompanied by his paramour, Minky Maloney, has returned for a brief visit to his domain, the newsroom. All seems well. The plane wreck is destined for the top of Page One, the crucifixion is a one-line brief on Page Six based on wire copy. AP just sent an alert that they're preparing something about the Filibuster's star sports columnist, Mutt Prescott.

"Look at this, Minky — Mutt must have won another award."

"Funny time to tell us — late Friday night," said Minky.

"Well, not ours to reason why AP does things," said Chutney

"They themselves don't know." Minky chuckles.

Now Vipes sees Chester Bontemps enter the newsroom. Chester's blond hair is rumpled, his eyes are watery and he seems to be moving very slowly.

"Hello, Chut," Bontemps says. "I just found out about the crucifixion's being canceled."

"It wasn't canceled, Chet," said Vipes. "We've got a wire story that says they just finished them off and tore down the crosses."

"No, I mean our coverage was canceled. I just saw Caninski's memo. I'm shocked and depressed. We're behaving like a public relations firm, not a first-class newspaper."

Chester shuffled toward his office.

"Doesn't he know?" Minky snickers.

"Know what?" says Chutney.

"We're not a first-class newspaper!" There is a glint in Minky's eyes as she announces, "We ARE the biggest PR firm in town."

"Speak no heresy, woman." Vipes laughs.

"It's our secret, Chut."

The phone rings, and Vipes picks it up.

"Detroit Filibuster, Vipes. . . Oh, hi, Dave. . . Yes, I got your memo. Everything is taken care of . . . Don't worry, Dave."

Dave Caninski is alone in the cottage his family shares with the Pilates. He sometimes retreats to this lakeside hideaway when he wants to reflect alone. Tonight, he has wasted a few precious minutes tearing some moronic real estate agent's "FOR SALE" sign out of the yard, but now he's buckling down to work.

Caninski is in the middle of a new version of his Sunday column in which he is writing frankly about Herod's attempt to blackmail him, using Mutt Prescott as a hostage. He is just now trying to decide whether to write equally frankly about his onetime willingness to let the king coerce and extort him. However, his decision regarding whether to mention the cause of his change of heart about reporting the crucifixion — namely, revenge on Herod for his crude jabs at the "two bad lays" sign — is already made. For legal if not moral reasons, it would be unwise to concede in print that revenge is a motivating factor at the Filibuster.

Suddenly, it occurs to Caninski that he should make sure Vipes received his change of instructions. And there was the matter of Chut's memo of contrition, in which he outlined several punitive measures to be taken against his nemesis, Rob Wolfman.

Caninski places a call for Vipes and for once reaches his city editor. "Just so you know, Chut, I read your note about Wolfman and am duh enormously disappointed by the duh tone of your recommendation and by the recommendation itself. You propose these phony duh therapy sessions so you can duh clobber the man mentally. You're missing the duh point, Chut. You want to duh control this man, you don't torture him. No, Chut, you make him a duh star. Give him what all duh reporters dream about. You want him to work overtime at your duh beck and call? You want him to write the duh stories you want, not what he likes? You want him to toe your duh line? Here's what you do: Give him duh plum assignments, Chut; put his stories at the top of Page One duh no matter if they turn out to be pap. Help him win some dumb-ass awards. Make his name a duh household word, or at least, duh, make him think so.

"You make him a star, Chut. Stardom is the straightest path to slavery there is.

"And by the way, Chut, how's the crucifixion?" asks Caninski.

"I'm following your orders to the letter," says Vipes. *Rob Wolfman a star?* Vipes wants to throw up.

Caninski hangs up the telephone, secure in the knowledge that Filibuster reporters, editors and photographers are slamming together a first-class journalistic effort at covering the events on Calvary Hill.

In the Gethsemane Bureau, Bob Saunter is still at work long past quitting time. Truth to tell, however, he isn't hard at work on Filibuster reporting. He is working on his sarcastic little manual, "Mine Comp," explaining how to turn editors' primal fear of paying overtime wages into weeks and even months of invisible-on-the-budget compensatory time vacations by means of subtle fraud and veiled intimidation.

Like Caninski, Saunter has interrupted his work to have a little telephone chat. But unlike Caninski, Saunter's conversation is with a soldier from the enemy army — a reporter on the News and Free Press.

Through the newspaper grapevine, Saunter now knows that the Filibuster's rival paper has just dumped its crucifixion package — off-track, anyway, since its lone reporter wandered away in quest of a pump — to make space for a late-breaking story about the Filibuster's ace columnist, Mutt Prescott.

Saunter looks across his desk at Daley Strumm, who is rapidly typing a long story about the crucifixion, occasionally stopping to discuss the event with his chief source, a chap named John. Saunter decides it isn't a good time to interrupt Daley with gossip about Mutt Prescott, the universally reviled Filibuster writer whose salary is rumored to be nearly equal to that of — gasp! — Chester Bontemps.

Yet the gossip is too good to hold back. Not only is Mutt Prescott in jail, booked on a charge of soliciting a prostitute, but the New Imperial Times wire has a story saying the Filibuster had been financing Mutt's sexual forays and that Caninski himself may be implicated. The Times is quoting Caninski as having exclaimed, "I've never had two bad lays in a row!" And AP has Caninski almost admitting it: "How many whores have we paid?"

Saunter decides the person who most deserves to know about this gossip, which he assumes to be gospel, is Rob Wolfman. He is about to punch Wolfman's number into his telephone. Just then, the phone rings. Saunter recognizes the voice and marvels. The voice does not identify, but Chutney knows who it is. Caninski. David Caninski, publisher, calling the godforsaken Gethsemane Bureau?

"Give me duh Daley Strumm," Caninski says.

"Please," says Saunter.

"Duh pardon me?"

"You forgot to say please."

"Don't coach me in duh manners! Give me Daley Strumm!"

"Daley," Saunter says without covering the phone, "There's a rather rude person on the line who wants to have a word with you."

Furious, Caninski explodes, "Come! How's it strumming?"

Silence. Now Caninski is really pissed. He senses that these bureau rats, these zoneheads, these miserable exiles to the farthest reach of the Filibuster circulation area, are treating him as an equal or worse, as a buffoon with an overinflated ego. A corner of his brain replays his words. He perceives his error, an honest though silly mispronunciation. For an instant — a mere instant, no more — he feels, for once in his life, like an idiot. It doesn't last. Burn your bridges, he thinks. Act like it didn't happen and perforce, it didn't.

"Strumm duh duh Strumm," says Caninski, and suddenly, the word "guitar" pops into his head. Why are these mistakes coming out of his mouth? Is he being played by these third-rate hacks? Move on, move on, pretend it's not happening.

"Strumm! How's that duh crucifixion story coming?" Caninski soldiers on.

"Oh, it's coming just fine. I've had some very good luck. I met Barabbas while I was in jail and I've got John helping out."

Those names mean nothing to Caninski. One dread word clicks. Shades of Mutt!

"You were duh in jail?" Visions of another scandal rise in front of Caninski's eyes. "What for?"

"Animal cruelty, but it isn't true. Anyway, the deer escaped. And while I was in there, I met Jesus. Well, not exactly. He came to me in a sort of vision."

"Jesus H. Christ, Strumm, you can't report on a vision! Next thing, you'll be using tarot cards, Ouija boards and all that duh duh duh dumb shit. Tell me about the duh crucifixion. How was it? You get near enough to talk to Jesus while he was on the cross? What kind of quotes you get?"

"Well, I had a slight problem, because I was in jail during most of the crucifixion. As I say, Jesus did come to me in a sort of visitation, although he was on the cross at the time. And he spoke to me."

"Duh you can't use that shit, Daley! This is a newspaper, not a tent revival. So you blew the assignment completely."

"No. I have a source who was a witness to the entire crucifixion and who took excellent notes on everything that happened, including what Jesus said. He's here with me now, and he's sharing his memories and his notes with me."

"God, duh that's a relief, Daley. It's hearsay, of course, and wouldn't duh stand up in court, but we're not lawyers, duh, are we? Who is this duh source, a cop?"

"No, he's a follower of Jesus — one of the twelve disciples."

"What! You're duh using an interested party as a source? Daley, duh I can't tell you how duh disappointed I am in you. Your sense of ethics is duh shallow indeed, if you think you can duh foist a biased observer on the duh reading public as if he were some kind of duh official source for your duh story. What duh credentials does this man have?"

"His credentials are that he was there and saw what happened."

"Not duh good enough. We need police, duh prosecutors, duh judges — official people with official duh titles. Doesn't matter if they know anything. This is Journalism CI, Daley! Elementary. You duh make some calls to that type of source, and don't try to duh palm off duh any disciples of Jesus on this newspaper, because we are too duh good for that, Daley. Too damned good."

So ends Daley Strumm's inspirational conversation with David Caninski. Daley sets the phone down, looks at John and shrugs. He will not call any officials. If Dave wants that work done, he can do it himself.

Daley returns to writing. With John.

Now, just as good reporters have an instinct, a sixth sense, that makes them almost naturally gravitate toward stories, so editors have an attraction, an invisible field of force, that helps them locate other editors.

This is the only way we can explain how Don Strodum knew where to find Caesar O'Toole. Unless, of course, he looked up bars, saloons and lounges in the Yellow Pages under the assumption that the first place to look for an errant editor is in a swill joint.

When Don Strodum walks into Iscariot's, he sees the bar littered with the dead bottles of various expensive imported beers. Caesar O'Toole, oblivious, is alone. In fact, O'Toole is sound asleep on the bar. The pages of his grand design for winning a Pulitzer Prize lie scattered on the bare wooden floorboards.

Strodum picks up the sheets and begins reading Caesar's glowing report on the successes of Strumpff and Strumm at Calvary. Strodum smiles. All for naught, of course. How would he break the news to poor Caesar that he'd wasted this trip to Gethsemane? How could he tactfully inform the junior editor that the crucifixion story had been scrubbed? O'Toole is sleeping very soundly — that gives Don some time to think. He feels sorry for the poor fellow.

Strodum makes his way to the cooler, and after a thorough search, his thoughts drift away from O'Toole's predictable disappointment at the cancellation of CROSS and begin dealing with more pressing issues.

Turning toward the recumbent O'Toole, Don Strodum bellows, "Caesar, you asshole! You drank up all the beer!"

Jack Quinine, music critic on the Filibuster, once said, "If it's true that computer terminals cause cancer, it's nice to know the editors who sit all day glued to the things will be the first to go."

Back on the Filibuster city desk, one of these future oncological patients opens a long story named CROSS with Daley Strumm's byline. The editor, a thin man named Will Barrett, is so impressed with the story that he calls several copy editors over for a look. Barrett invites them to read what he terms "an example of world-class journalism." After everyone in the newsroom has looked and admired, Barrett notes that the city editor, Chutney Vipes, has ordered that no trace of crucifixion coverage be left in the Filibuster computer, on orders of Caninski.

Barrett pushes a computer key marked SPIKE, sending Daley's story to that particular hell set aside for news stories that don't make print.

chapter XXX

FRESH AND NEWLY ALIVE

At six ante meridian on Saturday morning, the downtown streets of Detroit are nearly free of traffic. One car, a black Cadillac, is weaving back and forth along Woodward Avenue as its driver, a rotund little man, punches buttons on his cellular telephone with the fingers of his right hand while holding the phone with his left. At this instant, he is trying to steer with his right elbow.

David Caninski is feeling fresh and newly alive. Before turning in last night, he read Strumm's crucifixion story on his computer. It is excellent. Jam-packed with enormously, indeed profoundly significant facts, yet emotionally moving. Relentlessly interesting. A tad overly reliant on the biased source, John, but the Pulitzer judges would never notice. All the marks of a prize-winner, yet a great read over a long Saturday breakfast. Daley deserves special praise for his effort, and Caninski intends to tear off a front page of the Filibuster and pen one of his raves and send it out to Gethsemane by special courier. Why not? He used to send bonuses to Mutt Prescott by courier. Of course, that was before. Why, he could do even more. He has Daley Strumm's home telephone number. He would call him bright and early on Saturday morning and tell him, personally, man to man, what a true genius he is.

First, though, he has to say a few words to Chutney Vipes, who'd had a pretty rough day following through on the crucifixion story.

Oh, what a struggle to get this phone dialed! He weaves the big car down Woodward Avenue, and tries to concentrate. You have to hold the telephonic instrument in your left hand and punch the number buttons with your right while all the time attempting to steer the big automobile on a steady course, letting go with your elbow and now using your knees to hold the wheel.

Finally, the call rings through to Vipes' home. Chut answers.

"Chut," says Caninski. "I want to duh congratulate you on a magnificent performance under adverse duh circumstances with your job on the crucifixion. I read the fine piece by Daley Strumm at home last night and duh must say that I never knew the man had such compassion, such duh warmth. Or at least duh he certainly knows how to convey those duh feelings in writing."

Caninski stops talking, waiting for Chut to offer some genuflecting reply. But there is silence at the other end.

Out of the corner of his eye, Caninski notes two quite normal pieces of the Detroit street landscape. One is a blue-and-orange Detroit News and Free Press vending machine. He can see the top half of a newspaper with a heavy black banner headline, "MUTT MUFFS!" Well, that comes as no surprise. Herod was bound to have his revenge, and there it is. The rival paper is having lots of fun with old Mutt's downfall. Well, Caninski has toughed it out through stormy public relations scenes before — that's why they paid him in solid gold buckos and not the shrieking pigs and stinking goats payroll hands out to reporters, photographers and copy aides.

But there is something out of sync about the second newspaper box. This one is bright red, a Filibuster box. Caninski feels as if he's stepped into a time warp. Maybe this machine didn't get serviced last night, except that isn't yesterday's Filibuster headline.

What? The top story in the Filibuster today is the airplane crash at City Airport!

Caninski's car screeches, stops, backs up. Its round, short-legged cargo hops out, bolts to the machine, fishes in his pocket for a special key, fits it in the slot, wrenches the door open and claws at the papers. He grabs twenty or thirty and hops behind the wheel. The Caddy roars, bouncing across potholes as its driver, tearing around a corner, obsessively flips through page after page while screaming at a dumbfounded Chutney Vipes.

"Chut! Duh where's the crucifixion? Where the hell is it?"

Chutney Vipes is standing in his kitchen with a piece of unbuttered toast cooling in his left hand. He holds the phone to his right ear and listens as the publisher curses, invoking Jupiter, Mars, Mithras and Jehovah, then falls silent, leaving the phone to pick up and transmit the sound of the car's transmission shifting, the pages rustling, and then more cursing.

"Duh I can't find our crucifixion stuff anywhere!"

What comes next sounds to Chutney like a bomb exploding, a big BOOM followed by the squeal of metal grating on metal and glass raining on concrete. There is a long silence, then Caninski's voice, sounding weary, beleaguered, comes back.

"Goddam, Chut, duh — two bad days in a row."

END

ABOUT THE AUTHOR

Joel Thurtell was a Peace Corps volunteer in Togo, West Africa, and a newspaper reporter for 30 years. He was editor of The (Berrien Springs) Journal Era and a staff writer with the South Bend Tribune and Detroit Free Press.

His account of canoeing a polluted Detroit river, *Up the Rouge!*, was chosen by the Library of Michigan as a Michigan Notable Book for 2010.

He wrote *Shoestring Reporter: How I Got To Be A Big City Reporter Without Going To J School and How You Can Do It Too*, as a how-to manual for journalists.

Thurtell's blog, joelontheroad.com, was named "best independent blogger raising hell" by Detroit's Metro Times newspaper.

CPSIA information can be obtained at www.ICGtesting.com
Printed in the USA
LVOW070900191111

255722LV00002B/169/P